Ralph Fozbek
and the Amazing
Black Hole Patrol

Other Avon Camelot Books by
Steve Senn

THE DOUBLE DISAPPEARANCE OF WALTER FOZBEK

STEVE SENN was born in Americus, Georgia, and grew up in a small southern town whose main industry was producing peanut butter. He attended Ringling School of Art in Sarasota, Florida, and presently lives in Jacksonville, Florida, where he works as an art director. He also paints pictures and writes books, including the Avon Camelot, THE DOUBLE DISAPPEARANCE OF WALTER FOZBEK.

Ralph Fozbek
and the Amazing
Black Hole Patrol

Written and illustrated by

Steve Senn

AN AVON CAMELOT BOOK

AVON BOOKS
A division of
The Hearst Corporation
1790 Broadway
New York, New York 10019

Text and illustrations copyright © 1986 by Steve Senn
Published by arrangement with the author
Library of Congress Catalog Card Number: 86-1146
ISBN: 0-380-89905-1
RL: 6.4

Library of Congress Cataloging in Publication Data

Senn, Steve.
   Ralph Fozbek and the amazing black hole patrol.

   (An Avon Camelot book)
   Summary: Ralph is not looking forward to a boring summer until the night
Dr. Krebnickel's Black Hole escapes from his laboratory and he assists in the
recovery, causing such wild misadventures he welcomes the end of it.
   [1. Black holes (Astronomy)—Fiction.   2. Science—Fiction]   I. Title.
PZ7.S474Ral   1986   [Fic]   86-1146

First Camelot Printing: July 1986

Contents

Ralph Fozbek
and the Amazing
Black Hole Patrol

1 : Abandoned
in Fogville

BORING, boring, boring.

That's what Ralph Fozbek thought as he tried to go to sleep that June night. It was going to be a boring summer for him. His cousin Walter was on vacation with his parents at the Grand Canyon. And after that, Walter was going to Mexico. Fiestas! Pyramids! Aztecs and Spaniards fighting for pagan treasure! And here was Ralph, trapped in Fogville. He never got to go anywhere. He wiggled his toes way down in the sheets in frustration.

Only last year, his cousin Walter had gone on a *real*

adventure. Thanks to the scientific goof-ups of Dr. Kreb-nickel, Fogville's daffy genius, Walter had visited another whole universe. One with dinosaurs in it instead of humans. He had met triceratops kids! Tyrannosaurs! Walter had even tried to get back to his own universe by going through a black hole the professor had trapped. Ralph still had the H32 helmet Walter had worn to protect himself. Dr. Kreb-nickel had let Ralph keep it as a souvenir. Now is was just sitting there on his desk, a reminder of how boring his life was.

And Ralph was stuck in this universe, the dull one, about to be abandoned in Fogville. Even Dr. Krebnickel was going on vacation, as soon as he sold his new neutrino turbine to the Metro Power Agency. The professor was going to Europe. To Switzerland, to give a speech at the Einstein Museum. There would be no Krebnickel adventures this summer.

Maybe he could build a model of the Great Pyramid out of sugar cubes in his backyard. Nah. It would rain, or the ants would get it. Maybe this was the summer to start his science project: The Effect of Gamma Rays on Tuna Casserole.

Boring.

He could always hang around with Ray Chooka and his gang, the Junkyard Rats. They would try to get him to steal car batteries with them. Or filch cigarettes from their older brothers and smoke them in the park, then get caught by the older brothers, who were even nastier than the Junkyard Rats. Then get killed.

Ralph preferred being bored to getting killed, as a rule.

He drifted off to sleep, thinking of his boring future.

He had a very boring dream, about pancakes that he had to cut up with a chain saw. Only the chain saw wouldn't work. He sogged around in maple syrup, trying to start the saw and wondering why he was here. Then things slowly started getting brighter. The pancakes were on fire! His chain saw had turned into a fire extinguisher, but it still wouldn't work.

"Wait a minute," Ralph said. "It's not a fire. My room is bright."

He sat up. Blue light bathed everything. He squinted. Something on his dresser was really bright . . . the H32 helmet! The souvenir of Walter's trip into the black hole. It was as bright as a light bulb. And . . . hovering?

It was hovering, all right. Just inches above his dresser, but rising slowly, like a balloon filling with helium. It rose into the air and floated into the middle of the room.

Then his room gave a wobble. It wasn't just the helmet—the whole house felt like it was floating!

"Yulp!" Ralph gasped. He had just realized he was suspended just an inch or two above his bed, weightless.

Slowly, the glowing H32 helmet started moving. It drifted in a wandering way toward Ralph's open window, and before he could decide what to do, it had floated outside. It left as if it were a sleepwalker summoned by a magician's flute.

Ralph flailed around, trying to fight his way out of the sheets. At last he floated free of them, or maybe they floated free of him. Anyway, he found the floor with his toes, but there was no gravity to hold him there. When he tried to walk, he rotated like a pinwheel.

He yulped again, and flapped. That helped a lot. He

traveled in the direction he was flapping, awkwardly. He was swimming! But air was a lot thinner than water. He glided into the wall.

Then he paddled to the window. There was the H32 helmet, escaping gradually from the yard. Ralph looked down. The yard was a lot further away than it should have been. In the moonlight, he could see the shadow of the house bobbing on it.

Suddenly he realized he was in the middle of a real, honest-to-God mystery! And if he didn't get the helmet back, he might never figure out what was happening. Or worse—lose the proof that anything had happened at all. But how could he get the helmet back? Swim after it? Ralph gulped. A grappling hook, maybe?

There was his Scout camp robe, floating nearby. And slowly the coat hangers were drifting out of his closet, dancing his clothes across the floor. He grabbed one out of a jacket and tied the rope to it. Now, if he could just hook that helmet, or even reach the ON switch, maybe he could reverse this crazy process. When you flipped the switch, the helmet generated a field that protected you if you went inside a black hole—maybe it had gotten turned on somehow.

The hanger wobbled out of the window, rolling in the moonlight. It missed the helmet, but didn't fall. He yanked it back, and it rattled off the H32 helmet as it returned. He threw again. This time the hook of the coat hanger grappled the helmet's two antennas. They buzzed. The helmet grew brighter.

Ralph squinted, and started hauling in. But instead of reeling in the helmet, he was just pulling the house closer to it! The helmet was still making its way over the trees, towing the Fozbek house.

He pulled harder. That made one corner of the coat hanger dip and touch the top of the helmet.

BAM! *Flash!*

Like a strobe light going off, the flash blinded Ralph for a second. But he could feel the helmet dropping straight down. Then the Fozbek house followed it.

"Yuuuuuuuuullllllllpppp!!"

Right after the house landed in the yard with a horrible crash, everything in his room hit the floor. Especially Ralph. When he caught his breath, he found that his room was in one piece. The house was even in one piece. All the lamps had fallen over, and none of the pictures had stayed on the walls. But the walls were okay, and the roof, too.

Just then Ralph heard his father roar. His sister Dolly was crying. His mother was making a regular noise, like hiccups, only a lot louder. Everybody was thumping around like elephants.

Suddenly his door exploded open. "Ralph! My baby! Are you all right? HIC!" His mother tried to hug him, but stumbled and fell over his telescope.

He helped her up, and they both followed the sound of Papa's roaring into the kitchen.

"EARTHQUAKE! It's a quake, I said!" he was shouting into Dolly's toy telephone. "HELLO, OPERATOR?" When he realized his mistake he snorted like a bull and yanked the real phone from the wall.

"Wait a minute!" Ralph yelled. "That wasn't an earthquake!"

"It wasn't?"

"No. This isn't California!"

Ralph's father blinked. "Oh." Then his eyes grew wider. "The Russians! It's them. It's terrorists! OPERATOR? Get me the Defense Department! I want the Bureau of Sabotage! What? I most certainly am NOT drunk! My house was just bombed by Russian terrorists! Hello? Hello? OPERATOR!"

Papa growled at the telephone. Just then a pot fell onto the microwave oven, and everybody jumped.

"Albert," Mom said, "do you think they—HIC!—got the rest of the neighborhood?"

Everyone trooped out the front door, once Papa had pounded it open. There was no front walk anymore, so Ralph's whole family stumbled out onto the damp grass to see how badly the Russians had hit the rest of the houses.

But the street looked normal. Everything was quiet. All the other houses were right where they should be. The Fozbek house wasn't. It rested on the grass about fifty yards from its square foundation, as if the whole building had taken a big hop.

Wow, Ralph thought. The H32 helmet packed a lot of power.

Papa made a noise. It was sort of a cross between a groan and a whoop. His eyes were bugging out, staring at the empty foundation. They helped him inside, and Mom hunted around for the insurance agent's telephone number. Papa just sat on the sofa and mumbled about Russians, and earthquakes, and coverage.

Things settled down a little after Mom reached the agent. He was her cousin Wiley, and he told her everything would be all right. Papa seemed to relax then. Mom saw Ralph and Dolly back to their bedrooms, and tucked them in.

It was real late. But Ralph waited awhile anyway, just to make sure everyone was asleep. Then he got his clothes on and slipped out of the window. He found the H32 helmet in the Johnsons' hedge. It wasn't glowing anymore. It wasn't even warm. It gave no hint of what had happened to it in the darkness of his room. He stuck it under one arm carefully and crept away.

There was only one person in Fogville who was likely to know how to solve the mystery . . . Dr. Ladislav Krebnickel. And Ralph had to reach him before the professor left town.

2 : The Runaway Hole

BY the time Ralph got to the top of the hill on Mars Road, he was pretty sure something had changed Dr. Krebnickel's summer plans too. The dark line the professor's house made against the lights of the expressway was quite different tonight. And the fog in the air smelled smoky. The closer he got, the more he was sure that the mystery had spread beyond just the Fozbek property. There were boards all over Dr. Krebnickel's lawn.

The third time Ralph rang the bell, the porch light came on. The door opened and the professor appeared, looking around blearily. Dr. Krebnickel was wearing his lab coat, but it was all sooty. One sleeve was gone.

"Ralph! What are you doing here?"

"Doc! W-what's happened?"

The professor glanced down the street nervously and yanked Ralph inside.

"Oh, it's perfectly awful, Ralph! Cataclysmic! Look what's happened to my wonderful house."

Ralph looked. There was a big hole in the floor. Right in the hall, bigger than Ralph-size. Bigger than Krebnickel-size. It was hippo-size. Steam or smoke or something was

coming out of it from the laboratory beneath. Then Ralph looked up.

There was a hole in the ceiling, too. And above that, in the roof. Stars showed through at the top.

"There's a hole all the way through your house!"

Professor Krebnickel just made a whining noise and clambered down the stairs to the basement lab. "The turbine . . . my beautiful turbine . . ." he whimpered.

The lab was a wreck. Dr. Krebnickel had made a big pile of most of the broken stuff in one corner. But soot was still everywhere, coating all the flasks and computer terminals. Even Dr. Krebnickel's computer, named Quarwyn, was coated with a smoky layer. Electrical wires had been tossed around like spaghetti. In the center of the room was the neutrino turbine.* Or what was left of it. The big curtain that circled it now hung in tatters. Lots of pipes and Plexiglas tubes poked up toward the hole in the ceiling, blackened.

"Everything is smashed!" Dr. Krebnickel whined. "Now I cannot demonstrate the turbine to the power agency. How my greatest enemy, Fairfax Heminglas, will gloat! Just look at the damage!"

"Wow," Ralph said. The H32 helmet dropped from his grip and rattled on the floor.

Dr. Krebnickel flinched, as if it were going to explode too. Then he recognized it. "The helmet! The old one I let you keep last year—why did you bring it?" The professor blinked. "As a matter of fact, why are you here at all, at

*See Krebnickel's Glossary

this hour? Don't tell me you heard the explosion!"

"No. Something weird happened at my house too, Doc. The H32 helmet floated right off the ground! Honest. And that's not all. The whole house took off with it," Ralph explained. "Then, when I tried to get the helmet back, everything fell down."

"Mmmmmm," Dr. Krebnickel muttered thoughtfully. "Umm-hummmm. Gravity waves. Of course, that's what it would be. They temporarily canceled out the earth's pull in your vicinity."

"Gravity waves? But where did they come from?"

"Oh, no mystery at all about that." The professor began toeing a layer of broken glass into a pile on the floor. "No. The hole would have caused that, when it escaped."

"Your black hole* escaped again? The one you use to power the turbine?"

"Not really escaped. No, no. That's the mystery. You see, the jar holding it cracked. I was winding down the last experiment. Everything had gone perfectly. The turbine was ready to present to Metro Power. Then . . . the power source localizer just broke free of the machine."

Ralph knitted his brows. "Power source localizer? You mean that old pickle jar you rigged up to hold the hole?" It was really spooky, the way the doc had captured a black hole and kept it in his laboratory.

"Yes. Ordinarily it is fully protected by the X web I generate around it. But that didn't help a bit in this case.

*See Krebnickel's Glossary

The jar just wobbled up out of its mooring. It floated right up and cracked against the ceiling."

"Hey, that sounds just like what happened at my place!"

"Ya. The gravity waves from the hole could have caused your occurrence. But what made my power source localizer levitate? Could there be a cosmic generator hidden somewhere in this city?" Dr. Krebnickel grew thoughtful.

"What happened after the jar started floating?" Ralph urged.

"KA-BOOOM!" the professor said. His arms indicated turbulence.

"It exploded?"

"Dear me—no. Not exploded. When the jar cracked, the hole left immediately for its native space—out near Andromeda.* It was traveling at what appeared to be several times the speed of light. My house just got in the way."

Ralph whistled. It was a good thing the hole had been going so fast. Any slower, and its massive gravity might have torn the whole house up. Even all of Fogville, maybe.

"As it left, it generated gravity waves. One must have picked up your house for a moment."

"It got the H32 helmet first." Ralph shrugged. "Made it glow. That's what woke me up."

"Ya," Dr. Krebnickel mumbled, "the helmet. WHAT? You mean, the H32 helmet actually *glowed?*"

"Yeah. Bright blue. Before I noticed everything was floating."

*See Krebnickel's Glossary

Just then they heard a noise at the basement window. Following it, they saw a small head observing them. It wore glasses and a grin.

"Louie!" Dr. Krebnickel gasped.

It was Loony Louie. Ralph groaned. Louie was a nerd. A spectacular nerd. But he was the smartest kid in Dr. Krebnickel's Science Club.

The smartest kid in the Science Club lost his grip and tumbled through the open window.

"Yoooooorrrrrkk!" Loony Louie slid into a data bank. He bounced off it and landed flat on the floor.

As they helped him up he nearly dropped the blackened frazzled object he was carrying.

"Louie," Ralph said, "your face . . . it's all sooty. What's *that?*"

"It was my science project," Louie said. "Boy, Professor, it looks like your lab blew up just like my gravity gauge!"

"Ya," the professor said, wiping his brow. "It got pretty messy . . . your *what?*"

"My gravity gauge. It was almost ready to show to you. Then, about midnight, it blew the door off my closet. Wham! Boy, were my parents excited!"

"*What is going on?*" Ralph said. "Boy! Floating houses, exploding gravity gauges, escaping black holes!"

"I am sure we can get to the bottom of this," Louie said calmly. "Perhaps Quarwyn can be of some assistance."

"Yeah," Ralph said. It was Quarwyn, the big crystal computer, who had helped out with Walter's problem last summer. "Let's ask Quarwyn."

Dr. Krebnickel threw up his hands. "Alas! Alas! I have

been unable to reach Quarwyn since the accident. I am afraid the gravity must have damaged his circuits. From what Ralph tells me, I believe some force has been tampering with my X-web equipment. It made his H32 helmet actually glow, which means that what happened at his house took place before my hole escaped. The same force must have destroyed your device. I have no way of knowing where the force is coming from. All is lost. No contract from the power agency. No vacation."

"Hey, wait a minute!" Louie waved his arms. "Is this the same Dr. Krebnickel who discovered the wimpflush principle? The inventor of the transgnomic feeper?"

Dr. Krebnickel didn't deny it, though he looked as if he wished he could.

"Well, then," Louie insisted, "the Dr. Krebnickel I know isn't going to let a few stubborn circuits stand in his way. He's not going to let nasty old Dr. Heminglas laugh at him. Let's wake up Quarwyn!"

They pounded on Quarwyn's terminal. They shined lights up into the forest of quartz crystals that was the computer's main bank. That made pretty patterns on the ceiling, but Quarwyn did not wake up. Dr. Krebnickel whined. Louie punched heavy equations into a pocket calculator, then selected a precise place on one of the big crystals and tapped it with a pencil. Nothing happened.

Ralph stood to one side, since he didn't know much about science. He was thinking how late it was getting. Maybe they could solve the mystery tomorrow. His foot bumped into something, and he looked down as he kicked it out of the way.

"Hey, wait a minute," he said.

It was an electric plug. He put it in the wall outlet, and Quarwyn lit up like a Christmas tree.

"Hooray!" Dr. Krebnickel shouted. "Louie, you are a genius!"

"Simple, Professor. I just squared the ratio of molecular stress and triangulated the weak point. Nothing to it."

Ralph didn't even tell them he had been the genius who plugged the computer in. He stepped closer as Quarwyn woke up.

"Doctor! What happened? I detect a terrible ringing in my structure . . . Great vacuums! Your laboratory has been sacked! Was it the Vikings? Has there been a war?"

"Quarwyn," Dr. Krebnickel said, "the neutrino turbine—"

"SILENCE!" Quarwyn thundered. "Quarwyn can smell the answer! Gravity! Broken glass! The hole . . . the hole is free!"

"We *know* that!" Louie sniffed. "What we want to know is—"

"SILENCE," Quarwyn roared. "Professor, this looks like the same brat who spilled root beer into my transformer last Tuesday. Please keep him and his unpleasant little sculpture away from me while I solve this problem."

Louie protested, but Dr. Krebnickel made him take his blackened gravity gauge and stand behind a table. Ralph tired not to giggle.

"Bring the tachyphone," Quarwyn ordered.

Ralph helped Dr. Krebnickel attach wires to Quarwyn from a strange object made of coffee cans, coat hangers, and television picture tubes. "I forgot all about the tachyphone," Dr. Krebnickel explained. "Quarwyn communicates with black holes through it."

Ralph looked doubtfully at the device. "You mean this thing can send messages faster than light?"

"Oh, of course. But it cannot go *slower* than the speed of light. It sends tachyons* instead of radio waves."

Louie got all excited and started talking about mu mesons and other particles, but Quarwyn rumbled at him and he shut up again.

"Very well, Doctor. Dial the square root of 886-4933," the computer commanded.

It took a while for the professor to add that up, but at last he dialed the numbers on an old telephone dial set in the tachyphone. Quarwyn began glowing softly purple.

"Hello, Operator," Quarwyn said finally. "I would like to reach the party that lately inhabited Dr. Krebnickel's pickle jar. I believe it's Hole Number 5564-B. Yes, this is a collect call."

"Wait a minute!" Louie whispered. "You mean he can just call up a black hole on the phone?"

"Only this phone," Dr. Krebnickel confirmed. "And we can only call the answering service, at the Celestial Hole Union. They put us through to—"

"NO ANSWER?" Quarwyn growled. "Not at all? Are you sure the line is not busy?" In answer, the wires popped off Quarwyn's crystals. "She hung up. Hung up—on the world's oldest and greatest computer!"

*See Krebnickel's Glossary

Dr. Krebnickel gulped. "Now, Quarwyn, please stay calm."

Quarwyn wasn't listening. Sparks leaped between his crystals. Numbers raced across his terminal monitor. "We'll see about this," he thundered. "Doctor, up to the roof! Take the Fuzbek boy and the brat with the sculpture—you'll need all the help you can get."

"W-why, Quarwyn?" Dr. Krebnickel stammered as he herded the boys up the stairs. "What's your plan?"

"Simply to find that blasted wayward hole and bring it back to this laboratory! Then we'll see about black holes that don't answer the tachyphone."

"B-but—"

"TO THE ROOF!"

3 : Star Search

THE explosion had missed Dr. Krebnickel's telescope, Bertha. She was where she had always been, on a balcony that hung over the big oak tree in his yard. Ralph was the first one there. He had helped the professor with the big telescope lots of times. Loony Louie was back on the stairs, trying to convince Dr. Krebnickel that the hole's disappearance was caused by Halley's comet. Louie was big on comets.

"Really, Professor," Louie said, "check my figures."

"Later, Louie," Dr. Krebnickel said. "Right now we had

19

better find out where that hole is, or Quarwyn might get *really* mad."

Ralph chuckled. Then he laughed. "What could be worse than what's already happened tonight? You've got a hole right through your house!"

"What's worse?" Dr. Krebnickel said as he plugged things into the telescope. "Quarwyn's worse than any black hole when he's angry."

"Hmf," Louie said smugly. "It's just an old computer."

Dr. Krebnickel's telescope was really big. It towered into the sky. There were boxes and antennas all over it, and wires running down the stairs. It had a chair attached to it that swiveled with the scope. Sometimes, when Quarwyn was experimenting with gravity, things could get rough. Ralph helped the professor strap himself in and screw the funny-looking little binoculars onto his glasses.

"What are those?" Louie said loudly. And, "What is this? What does this thing do?"

"Those are infrared* analyzers," Ralph muttered. "And this is the X-web focal unit. *That* thing is a sponge soaking in milk of magnesia, to get the cosmic dust off if there's an implosion. Haven't you been up here before?"

Louie turned purple, an even funnier color by starlight.

"Actually," Dr. Krebnickel mumbled, "this is Louie's first visit with Bertha. He's an exceptional chemistry student, so he's mainly been in the lab."

"Yeah, exceptional." Louie nodded as he poked the old eggbeater crank that controlled Bertha's vertical swing.

Ralph snorted. He might not be so hot at science, but Dr. Krebnickel had needed his help lots of times with Ber-

*See Krebnickel's Glossary

tha. Ralph knew all about feeding the numbers into Quarwyn's terminal box. That way Dr. Krebnickel was free to handle all the physical problems of controlling Bertha.

"Ready, Professor?" crackled Quarwyn's voice over the communicator.

Dr. Krebnickel gulped and prodded the sponge. "Well, the milk of magnesia could be a little fresher . . ."

"BEGIN!" buzzed Quarwyn.

The circuits leaped into life. Bertha began bucking like one of those mechanical bulls, spinning this way and that. Dr. Krebnickel clung to the cranks desperately.

"Wow!" Ralph cried. "The gravity's driving Bertha crazy!"

"Sixteen degrees negative right ascension*—ulp!" Dr. Krebnickel shouted. "Twelve hours declination*!"

Ralph feverishly tapped the coordinates into the little computer on the porch. "Next!" he said.

"What are those numbers?" Louie demanded.

"Locations where there might be holes—" Ralph broke off as Dr. Krebnickel shouted another set of coordinates. He tapped them into Quarwyn's memory quickly. "The telescope can only locate strange gravity patterns. Quarwyn has to analyze them and identify them."

Louie dropped his wrecked invention. "You mean *that* thing is a gravity gauge?"

There was no time to answer. Dr. Krebnickel was swinging around and zipping up and down as Bertha's big eye scanned the universe over Fogville. He called off coordinates as he bounced, and Ralph typed them into Quarwyn as fast as he could.

Finally Bertha jumped and rattled to a halt, pointing to-

*See Krebnickel's Glossary

ward the Big Dipper. Dr. Krebnickel hung nearly upside down in the control seat. He gasped and panted. Quarwyn hummed.

"Wow, that was great!" Louie exclaimed. "You must have located every black hole in the sky."

"Just the big ones," Dr. Krebnickel wheezed. "And there are probably a few white dwarves* in the list, too."

"Seven white dwarves, exactly," Quarwyn said. "Twelve black holes, and a radio galaxy* turned up too high."

Dr. Krebnickel snapped off the infrared analyzers. "Is our hole on the list?"

There was a long pause quite unlike Quarwyn. "Possibly . . . There is something very strange. An object in Andromeda. But it doesn't seem to really exist."

"A black hole can't be seen," Louie explained eagerly. "Its gravity is so strong it won't even let light escape." He sounded like an encyclopedia.

"QUARWYN KNOWS THAT!" Quarwyn thundered. "Quarwyn is over four thousand years old, punk! *That* is no ordinary black hole. In fact, it's nothing. But it reads like ours, Professor. Let's go for it."

"Well, Quarwyn, you know, it's awfully late. Why don't we get some sleep and tackle this thing tomorrow—"

"PROFESSOR!"

"Ralph, man the auxiliary power puncher," Dr. Krebnickel gulped.

Ralph took the cover off the power puncher, which was an odd box with lots of wires and gizmos. He ignored Louie's questions.

---

*See Krebnickel's Glossary

"Ready, Professor," he said.

"Hey, wait a minute," Louie said. "I'm not ready! What's going on?"

Bertha began whining. Dr. Krebnickel had forgotten to replace his infrared analyzers, and he scrambled to get them on.

Louie continued, "Hey, Doc, what are you . . ."

Bertha coughed, hiccuped. Her whine got louder. Over the sound, Dr. Krebnickel could be heard praying in Latvian. The telescope swiveled up until it pointed at the constellation Andromeda, at the spot where Quarwyn said something wasn't. A mysterious non-something. When it had located the right spot, Dr. Krebnickel threw a switch made from an umbrella handle, and a beam of bright golden light shot out of the end of the telescope, reaching far into the night sky. The light sparkled and shimmered. Something like a slow wind curled around Dr. Krebnickel and the telescope. His clothes and hair fluttered.

Ralph was still ignoring Louie, though that was getting harder to do. The nerd was shouting in his ear. Finally Ralph felt a sharp pain in his shin.

"Hey! Don't kick me!"

"Well, *answer* me, then. What is that beam of light?"

"It's an X-web projector," Ralph said, as if that were perfectly obvious. "It uses a lure to attract black holes; then, when they're near enough, it grabs 'em with X beams."

"A lure? How can you lure a black hole?"

"It's a slide of Cyndi Lauper. I dunno. It seems to work. . . ."

Just then Bertha gave a lurch. Because she was bolted to the balcony, the balcony gave a lurch also. It was the biggest lurch Ralph had ever seen. It almost lurched them into the yard.

Dr. Krebnickel shrieked. Ralph thought he said, "There it is!" That meant that the hole had taken the bait.

He was right. Dr. Krebnickel stomped the pedal on the X-web focal unit, and Bertha gave another, smaller lurch. The X-web focal unit began glowing red and smoking. Ralph had never seen it do that.

Dr. Krebnickel shrieked again. This time Ralph thought he said, "Throw the switch!" Ralph did. The auxiliary power puncher stole six watts from every household in Fogville and pumped them into Bertha.

Then things really started happening—mainly in the air. That was where Ralph found himself, hanging on to the power puncher, his sneakers pointed at the stars. Upside down, he could see Dr. Krebnickel, clinging to Bertha and screaming. He was bright red and smoking. His hair was trying to get away from his head. Bolts and things were flying out of Bertha.

Ralph noticed the crazy gravity was pulling stronger on his left foot. He looked down, or rather up. There, against the stars, he saw Loony Louie holding on to his shoe, kicking and yelling.

"What's happening, Ralph?" Louie yelled. "What is that beam made of? Does it always do this?"

Ralph resisted the urge to wiggle his toes out of the sneaker. It would be great to see Louie disappear into the sky.

But there, beyond Louie, Ralph saw something coming. Or maybe nothing coming. It was a big black place, hurtling

down the X beam. Only Ralph had never seen anything this black, a black that didn't have any color in it at all. And it was eating the beam at the speed of light.

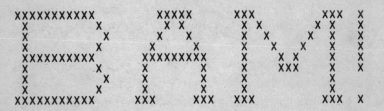

There was lots of wind, and then it began raining bolts and things. Ralph realized he was lying on the balcony floor. Then he realized Louie was sitting on top of him.

Dr. Krebnickel was a bundle of arms and legs hanging out of Bertha's seat. The little whirlwind that had been playing around the telescope spiraled down the machine and corkscrewed into an empty jar connected to the X box. It disappeared like a spiral of water down a drain.

The nothing was in the jar.

"Blecchhh," Louie groused. "What *is* this stuff?" He tried to wipe a scoop of gritty green stuff off his sleeve.

"Get off me!" Ralph said. He shoved Louie out of the way. Louie landed in a big pile of the green stuff.

"Blecchhh!"

The bundle of arms and legs that was Dr. Krebnickel twitched and mumbled something in Latvian about milk of magnesia.

They finally found the sponge in the debris. It didn't have much milk of magnesia left in it. Just enough to clean the cosmic dust from the implosion off their faces. Louie complained a lot. Then Dr. Krebnickel unscrewed the black jar out of Bertha's wreckage. On the way back downstairs, he tried to explain what had happened, but he didn't start speaking English until they were on the lab stairs.

". . . and then the accelerated gravity bonded a pion and three quarks, transferring the cosmic dust here. Messy and simple."

He might as well have kept speaking Latvian as far as Ralph was concerned. But he understood that the implosion had been a bad one. He had seen a cosmic dust fall before, but nothing like this.

Dr. Krebnickel held the jar up, beaming. "But we have the hole back! Let's take a reading, Quarwyn, before we hook it up to the turbine again."

Cosmic dust kept falling out of Louie's hair and clogging up his questions. But he watched closely as Ralph helped Dr. Krebnickel screw the jar into place on the scanner.

Dr. Krebnickel punched in some figures, and then Quarwyn threw a switch.

"Reading . . ." Quarwyn said.

"Yes?" said Dr. Krebnickel, poised with a pencil.

"Zero."

"Zero? That's impossible!"

"The jar appears to be dead, Professor. No field. No presence. But there appears to be . . . I think it's a time warp*."

Dr. Krebnickel sagged. "There goes my sale to the power agency!"

"What's the matter, Doc?" Louie said, wiping cosmic dust out of his mouth. "What happened to the black hole?"

*See Krebnickel's Glossary

"It tore through time. It's gone to another when. Now it cannot generate neutrinos to turn my turbine."

"It's too bad, Professor," Ralph said. He put one hand on Dr. Krebnickel's shoulder. It stuck to the cosmic dust.

"Wait a minute," Louie said suddenly. He was holding the H32 helmet, and he had a funny gleam in his eyes. "Maybe if the black hole won't come to us, we could go to the black hole."

"Ya, well that is poss—*What?* No! Absolutely not!"

"Aw, come on, Professor. One of us could just put on this helmet and zip right in there and fix it . . . me, for instance. I'm great at fixing things."

"I forbid it!"

"I forbid it too," Quarwyn chimed.

"Aw. Why?"

"Because they have brains," Ralph said. "Enough to know you don't mess around with a black hole, Loony."

Louie tried to argue, but Quarwyn's crystals began crackling sparks, and Dr. Krebnickel started talking in Latvian. Finally the professor put his foot down.

"Enough! As long as the jar is in a time warp, I cannot store another hole in it. And Bertha is in no shape to continue, even if I could. I will rebuild her, and the turbine, but now is the time for knowing when you're beat. There will be another meeting of the power agency, maybe, another time.

"And don't try any funny stuff, you two," Dr. Krebnickel called as they climbed the stairs. "Quarwyn will be on guard in the lab the rest of the night. Good night, boys."

4 : An Accidental Journey

THE trip home was very dark. This was the latest Ralph had ever been up, and he was tired of listening to Louie.

"It's really not that dangerous," Louie was saying as he pushed his bike along. "I don't see why Dr. Krebnickel won't let us visit the black hole." Louie's gravity gauge tapped against the handlebars as they walked.

"Just because," Ralph finally said. "Listen, my cousin Walter had a pretty rough time in that hole last year. And he didn't really even get to the hole itself."

"But we could." Louie said, ignoring him. "We could go in there and fix that old hole. I know we could. Just think,

Ralph. We'd be expanding the frontiers of science, going where no kid had gone before. What a strange, primitive place a black hole must be, like a little piece of the big bang, the explosion that started the universe."

"Just shut up, or I'll show *you* a big bang," said Ralph. "You're a nerd."

"And with the H32 helmet, no harm could come to us," Louie said. "Just set the coordinates of the jar, turn the switch on, and let the X beams suck you into the black hole. At the very least . . ."

That was the awful thing about Loony Louie. It was impossible to insult him. Ralph wondered if he should punch him. He decided it would be too much work. He just stopped listening instead.

Then something really strange happened.

At first it was just silly. The alarm clock attached to Louie's gravity gauge went off. Dogs started barking, and Louie frantically tried to shut it off. Then the gravity gauge floated up on its chain, pointing down Tallyrand Avenue.

"Holy smoke!" Ralph said.

"Look at that reading! Hey! My gravity gauge works!"

It really did. The needle was going crazy.

"What does that mean?" Ralph asked, peering closer.

"Gravity waves. Somebody is generating a big gravity field. And it's coming from over there. . . ."

Ralph saw a familiar tall chimney looming beyond the trees. "Dr. Heminglas!"

"You're right. That's his mansion over there. Hey, I bet he's behind what happened at Dr. Krebnickel's laboratory . . ."

"And at my house," said Ralph, remembering the floating H32 helmet, and what Dr. Krebnickel had said about a force from right here in Fogville causing it.

". . . and I'll bet he's the one who blew up my gravity gauge!" Louie said. "But that was probably by accident, and your floating H32 helmet was an accident too. Heminglas was trying to steal the doc's black hole!"

Nasty old Dr. Heminglas. There was only one reason he could be involved. He wanted the power agency contract himself. He was terribly jealous of Dr. Krebnickel. He had gotten rich stealing inventions from him. Now he was sabotaging Dr. Krebnickel's last chance for success.

"Ralph!" Louie said. "We've got to go back to the lab. We've got to fix that black hole so Dr. Heminglas doesn't win."

"You're crazy!"

"No, really. We can do it. Dr. Krebnickel's too tired to think straight. We can help him."

"I don't want to go into any black hole," Ralph protested. He was tired too. He wanted to be back in his bed, feeling bored.

Loony Louie wasn't listening. He was running back toward the lab. His gravity gauge was banging against the bike as he ran. And the H32 helmet was still strapped to the book rack.

Ralph moaned. He couldn't let a cosmic nerd like Louie wreck Dr. Krebnickel's lab again. He trotted after him, following the trail of cosmic dust.

"I'm going to be sorry I'm doing this. I really am," he mumbled to himself.

He really was.

When he got to the lab, wheezing for breath, Louie had already wriggled through the broken window. The lights were still on. Ralph peered in as Louie tried to tiptoe past Quarwyn's terminal with the H32 helmet. He was tempted to pick up a rock and bean him, but before he could do anything, a green light flickered through Quarwyn's forest of crystals. Great. Dr. Krebnickel had warned them he would leave the computer on guard.

"ALARUM!" Quarwyn's circuits rang. All his terminals blinked red.

Louie jumped straight up off the floor. "Qu-Quarwyn. Oh, hello. I—I forgot something."

"Of course you did. You forgot about me. Now get out of the professor's laboratory before I experiment with your molecules!"

"No."

"What?"

"I know exactly the place to strike you to turn you off. I computed it before, when I turned you on."

Ralph grinned in the dark. What a nerd.

"What? Strike *me?*"

Before Ralph could yell, Loony Louie whacked Quarwyn right in his biggest crystal with the helmet. Quarwyn didn't turn off. He turned orange. Then red. Louie started gurgling and backing up.

BAM! A bright yellow beam reached out of Quarwyn's main terminal and locked right around Louie's neck.

Louie went "Hgggggg!" His tongue shot out and his eyes

lit up all yellow. Quarwyn started tossing him up in the air, then batting him around like a Ping-Pong ball. Louie made funny noises.

As much as he was enjoying the show, Ralph figured he had to stop it. Quarwyn was going to wake up the professor, and then Dr. Krebnickel would get really mad, and maybe yell at them. Anyway, Ralph was a good member of the Science Club, and so was Louie. Ralph couldn't let anything happen to him.

Quarwyn didn't notice Ralph sneaking through the window and crawling across the floor. He did notice when Ralph pulled the big electric cord out of its socket again. Or rather, he stopped noticing anything. His terminals went black. The yellow beam frizzled out. Everything got quiet, except Louie. Louie squealed all the way to the floor, where he raised a big cloud of cosmic dust.

He sat up and coughed, then crawled over and picked up the H32 helmet. "That took longer than I thought to take effect," he said. "I should have hit him harder. Oh, hi, Ralph. I already deactivated Quarwyn. You can get up now. It's safe."

Louie spun a dial on the neutrino turbine, and lights went on around it. He turned the pickle jar in its housing until he could read the numbers on top of it.

"Louie, you're an idiot," Ralph growled as he climbed down. "Get away from that jar."

"But we can't go looking for the hole unless I do this." He punched the coordinates of the jar into the H32 helmet. That locked the helmet on course. A lavender light began blinking on it.

"Gimme that!" Ralph yelled. He snatched at the helmet, but Louie avoided the snatch.

"You're standing in the way of science!" Louie sniffed.

That did it. Ralph put his head down and rammed Louie right in his fat stomach. Or would have, if a test tube hadn't rolled out from under his foot. He hit Louie, but not solidly. He bounced off and he hit something Louie was holding.

BAM! The something whacked him on the head, then everything went dark. His head was inside it! It was the H32 helmet, on backwards! Suddenly, as he was trying to pull it off his head, his hand hit a button and it made a big click.

A *big* click.

5 : *Inside*

B
Z
  Z
   O
    I
    N
     N
      N
        NNNNNNNNGGG!!

The H32 helmet sucked him into the pickle jar, attracted to the vibrations of a black hole lost in a time warp. Ralph screamed.

It was like a bad elevator ride, made worse by having his nose flattened against the back of the helmet. He was hurtling through space so rapidly he felt his gravity increasing. He felt his molecules scrunching together as the helmet plunged him into strange realms beyond time and space. He was not bored. Maybe he would never be bored again.

He was protected from the gravity by the H32 helmet, but nothing could protect him from the horrible falling and squeezing feelings. It was very bad. Worse than the monster roller coaster in Feto City, the Bullet, that made pro wrestlers and astronauts throw up. Worse than having the flu *and* being on the Feto City Bullet, with Loony Louie driving.

FOOP!

Suddenly he landed in a sitting position on some kind of smooth surface, and skidded for quite some distance. When he stopped, he could breathe again. First he breathed, then he wrestled the helmet around so he could see.

He wished he hadn't turned the helmet around.

A small lavender person frowned at him.

The lavender person was sitting behind a desk littered with papers and staplers and stamps and IN and OUT boxes. He looked very official. On the corner of his desk was a wooden plaque that read GNORK, QUARTEXUS, TEMPORUM.

"Please, please, we haven't all the time in the world to settle your claim, now do we, sir?" the little person said. "May I help you?"

Well, here he was, in the black hole. It wasn't much like what he had imagined: crashing blue galaxies and X-ray blasts. It was some sort of building. Louie would never believe this.

"May I *help* you?" the lavender person repeated.

"Uh, yeah, I guess," said Ralph. All he could do now was play along.

"Excellent. We're getting somewhere. Please step away from the embarkation point."

Ralph looked behind him. Nothing was there. Just a black mist. Slightly damp. The dirty linoleum floor just ended and there was a wall of nothing. He gulped and stepped closer to the desk.

"Am . . . am I really inside a black hole?" he wondered aloud to the lavender person.

The lavender person blinked. "Of course you are. Hole Control Central, to be precise. The gravity core. Holes have to be very carefully monitored, you know, or the cheese would melt dreadfully. And at several times the speed of light, this hole is the fastest we've ever heard of."

"Cheese? Did you say *cheese?*" Ralph said.

"Of course. All space is merely potential cheese. And this is one of the holes. We're here to keep space from being melted by its holes."

Did that make sense? Ralph couldn't tell.

"Now, is this your first visit to Hole Control, sir? And as what may I address you?"

"Uh, Ralph. Ralph Fozbek. I come from Earth." The words sounded so *weird*.

"Of course," said the person, and he filled in Ralph's name on a form. "Doesn't everyone? Which Earth are you from?"

"How many are there?"

The man said a very long equation. It sounded like a lot. Then he gave a long sigh and put down his pencil. "I wish you people would get all this information before you come in here. It's Founder's Day, you know. Now. Is your Earth with or without pyramids?"

"With."

"Excellent. Quadrant 7, listing 645992XX." He wrote that down. "Now, what is your problem?"

"Um, well . . . I came here to see what happened to the black hole that powers Dr. Krebnickel's neutrino turbine. It went dead."

The lavender man rolled his eyes. They were bright green, with no whites. "That Krebnickel again! I must definitely notify the Bureau of Licenses. He doesn't have the authority to send a beginner into this place. And on Founder's Day!"

"Please don't blame Dr. Krebnickel. It was Louie's idea."

"Well, just tell him not to let you do it again. And tell him I'll be sending around a patrolman to talk to him in any event. We must do things in an orderly way. Just wait a moment and I'll send you inside."

"Inside" must have meant the door behind Mr. Gnork marked LORD GOMZTOOTH, HALL MONITOR. Ralph watched Mr. Gnork fill out two more forms, then staple them to a purple disk that looked a lot like a paper plate. He stamped the disk with three different stamps in different inks. The final product he rolled up and put in a cylinder, which was sucked away by a vacuum tube.

"Sign your name, please," Mr. Gnork said, pointing at a visitors' ledger. It had a column marked *Earth*. There were several names there already:

Aesop
Rabbi Akiba
Judge Crater
Charles Fort
A. Einstein

Ralph added his.

"You may go in now," Mr. Gnork said as he put on a funny-looking red hat. He turned off his desk light and flipped a sign around that said CLOSED. "Good day."

Ralph opened the door, gulping, and stepped inside. It was a waiting room, filled with people and creatures and colored shapes sitting around on sofas. Not many of them looked up. There was a hook on the wall beside his head with numbered cards on it. The sign above it said TAKE A NUMBER. Ralph's card was 78, but the card under it was 16. He decided not to reason it out, and sat down on a sofa next to an agreeable-looking panda wearing a cape.

The panda was talking to an octopus with a water-filled helmet. There were a couple of people waiting, and some sorts of creatures Ralph could recognize. An iguana in ballet tights sat next to a big pink armadillo. Beside the armadillo was a large rock with a numbered card stuck into one of its cracks.

A frog lady occasionally called a number through a window at the other end of the room, and somebody would get up and slither or hop or walk through another door. Sometimes two different people would have the same number and would have to go together. It didn't make any sense to Ralph. But then he guessed it didn't have to.

He tried reading some of the magazines, but most of them weren't in English. Some were not even rectangular. A giant sloth across the room was reading a cube. There was a round book on the table in front of Ralph, but it was written entirely in equations. It had very interesting pictures, though.

Something like *Treasure Island* with elephants. Ralph finally found an old *Mad* magazine and some church magazines and tried to read.

After a long time the frog lady called out, "Seventy-eight." Ralph handed her his card and went through the door. He was in another office, not much bigger than Mr. Gnork's, and just as dingy.

"Good day," said Lord Gomztooth. He was a big purple lizard. There was a long pink tail looping out around the corner of his desk.

"Hello," Ralph answered.

Lord Gomztooth was unrolling the disk with Ralph's papers stapled to it. "Ahh, I see we have another Quadrant 7 failure. Due no doubt to the special holiday we're having."

"Holiday?" Ralph wondered aloud.

"Hmmmm. Yes. Founder's Day. Whole place will be shut down for the occasion. Only happened once before, you know. The first time, when we were founded. Most of the staff has already left. Control is quite empty."

"But *you're* here."

"Just tidying up, lad. Many loose ends to fix up. Have to rush through all you visitors and get out myself. If only this hadn't come up so unexpectedly, things wouldn't be so . . . disorderly."

Ralph wondered how an anniversary like Founder's Day could come up unexpectedly. And who could the founder be, anyway? But he didn't say anything about those doubts.

"Why did Dr. Krebnickel's power go out, anyway?"

"A simple problem. Something on your side of reality generated an enormous gravity wave, which popped us right out of your professor's laboratory and into space."

"Dr. Heminglas!" Ralph gulped. "Trying to sabotage the professor's experiment."

"What? Oh, I have no way of knowing who did it, but whoever it was has certainly knocked us for a loop. A space-time loop, to be exact. We've crossed the time barrier, and now we're headed backwards."

"Is that why the power went dead?"

Lord Gomztooth wrinkled his nose. "No. When the gravity wave hit, it knocked out our circuit breakers. The janitors probably forgot to turn the duct switch back on, in the rush to get out. You could try to turn it back on, I suppose. But I don't know what good that will do you. It will be Founder's Day in just . . . forty-five minutes. Then everything will shut down."

"Oh, but let me try," Ralph insisted. "Louie expects results, and if I don't deliver, I might have to punch him out. I don't want to have to do that. Besides, I want to help Dr. Krebnickel."

"I really shouldn't let you in. Things are not exactly normal around here."

"I know," Ralph said. "Quarwyn said you were in a time warp."

Lord Gomztooth glanced sharply at him. His yellow lizard-eyes blinked. "Quarwyn? You know Quarwyn? Ohhhh . . . *that* Dr. Krebnickel. Of course. Why, that's different! We've known your friend Quarwyn for thousands of years. A fine fellow. Good sort. We've played chess by tachyphone. You know Quarwyn, eh? In that case, I think I could let you have a hall pass."

"That's great," Ralph said, grinning. Good old Quarwyn.

Lord Gomztooth shuffled around the room getting things from file cabinets, his long tail swishing. He handed Ralph a map, a folded black umbrella, and a key on a chain. The map was a diagram of a big building.

"You must go to the fuse-box station, which is on the roof," Lord Gomztooth explained, pointing to a spot on the map. "The Quadrant 7 box should be clearly marked. Just pull the switch down."

"What's the umbrella for?"

"I'm coming to that. The key will unlock the correct door

into Control. And the umbrella is for the flaming apes."

Lord Gomztooth sat down.

"The, ah, what, Your Lordship?" Ralph said.

"The flaming apes, boy. You'll no doubt encounter some on one of the floors. Our ventilation system is in bad need of repair, and when we have an ape shower they can fall through in places and burn up in our atmosphere. But use the umbrella and you'll have no difficulties. Remember, you have just forty-five minutes."

Ralph wanted to ask about the apes, but questions didn't seem like a good idea in this place. Lord Gomztooth wished him luck and pointed to a door. Then he leaned over and yelled for the frog lady to send in the next customer. Ralph gulped and stepped out into the hall.

When the door clicked shut behind him, he realized there must have been some mistake. Before him was a dark corridor, lined with about a thousand doors. Maybe a million. There were no labels on them to tell one from another.

Ralph turned around. But there was no wall behind him, and of course no door in it leading back into Lord Gomztooth's office. There was just the dark corridor, with about a million doors in it, stretching away.

He looked forlornly at the single key, and sighed.

6: Hot Cheese from Mars

THE corridor was so dark that he had tried the key in a dozen locks before he noticed the floor was transparent. He was standing on it, but he could see down dozens of half-lighted floors beneath him. It made him dizzy. He tried not to look down as he kept trying the key.

He was sweating inside the H32 helmet. He wondered how long he might be inside this crazy place, trying door after door. What if he needed help? Lord Gomztooth would be through with the last customer any time now, and heading home. He might be a lizard, but Ralph didn't want to be trapped in here without *anyone* else.

His sweaty hand made the handle of the key slippery. Then Ralph really looked at the handle, and noticed that it was glass. It looked like a lens. He wondered why, and he was glad Louie wasn't around to ask questions. On a hunch, he squinted through the handle, down the hallway at all the doors. There was a moment's fogginess, and then . . . all the doors but one faded away! He looked without the lens, and there were still a million of them.

It was showing him the right door! The lock clicked when he put the key in, but the door didn't open. It disappeared, just melted away.

Beyond was a darkened room, with what looked like rows of presses in it. As he stepped into the room a small machine in front of him made a whirring noise. Its lights blinked on. A drawer opened in it and a mechanical arm extended and a balloon on a string popped out. On the balloon was printed I'VE BEEN TO HOLE CONTROL.

The machine whirred again. "Thank you for visiting Hole Control, sir or madam. We wish you a safe return to your particular universe, and be sure to tell your friends how much you enjoyed your tour."

"Great," Ralph mumbled. He tied the balloon to his belt. Then, cramming the umbrella under one arm and the key in a pocket, he unfolded the map. He appeared to be in the Hole Press Room. That was what was marked next to Lord Gomztooth's office. And there were presses all around him. And he could make out stacks and stacks of different-size dark disks. Strangely, they were the color of his umbrella. Big disks were stacked beside the big presses, and small

disks were beside the others. Maybe they printed on disks, instead of paper. . . .

Then Ralph realized that he was looking at holes. The disks were holes, and the presses were actually manufacturing them. Too strange.

He plotted a likely course to the roof.

There was just enough light in the Hole Press Room for him to make his way safely to the exit. Beyond was a brighter office with carpet and lots of receptionists' desks. Potted plants were everywhere, orange and violet ones, but they stopped singing when he came in. According to the map, he was now in the Sales Office.

The elevators were on the floor above, and the map indicated there was some way to get there from the Sales Office. He couldn't tell for sure what that way was, because the instructions were in Spanish. He went through a glass door into a dark room. After some stumbling around he located the light switch.

He found himself in an open path between two groups of off-duty robots. They were all frozen like dummies, with big toothy grins and hands thrust forward in greeting. They all wore burgundy polyester suits and white shoes. There was a sign above them which read SALES FORCE 1X THROUGH 22X. They were salesmen.

All their glassy stares made Ralph feel uncomfortable. "Hi, guys," he said as he eased through the room. "Ralph's the name."

At the end of the Sales Force Room there was a tall escalator stretching up into darkness. Ralph pushed the button on its side and hopped on. The stairs vibrated a minute, and then started flowing *down*. He had to run up them just to stay ahead. But when he dropped his umbrella and turned around to pick it up, the escalator reversed directions! He tried turning around and discovered that whichever way he was pointed, the escalator took him the other way. He shrugged and faced the sales force until they receded further and further, and at last he was deposited on the floor above.

There were the elevators, four of them. Their tall doors reached from the floor to the ceiling high overhead, where there was a bright mosaic of the Marx Brothers. But halfway across the polished floor toward them, Ralph found a long trench barring his way. The floor just dropped away. He could see the lights of many levels of Hole Control down there, but he couldn't make out the bottom. And it was far too wide to jump across to the elevators. His heart sank. He couldn't possibly reach the elevators! There was no way to cross the trench.

The only way forward appeared to be a brass pole set a meter or so into the trench. Anchored in the ceiling, it disappeared into the darkness of the trench before him. It was like a fireman's pole. Whoever built this place was nuts. Ralph moaned. If he ever got out of this he would never complain of being bored again. There was nothing else he could do but continue on his way, and hope that the riddle of the elevators would clear up later on in his journey.

He stuck his umbrella through his belt like a sword, held his breath, and swung down the pole.

He fell in one long gulp down into the blackness. The brass pole squeaked through his hands faster and faster. Finally, lighted floors began flashing past. Ralph tried slowing down, but the pole was too thick. And he was going too fast. He got scared.

Just as he was ready to yell, he began slowing down automatically. The floors stopped flashing and began fluttering, then became individual floors. At last he came to rest on a carpeted floor. His knees were shaky, but he managed to find his way to a light switch.

Then he discovered he was not standing on carpet, but was ankle-deep in some powdery yellow material. He sniffed it, then tasted it.

"Cheese," he said. It was Parmesan cheese.

There was lots of it, all over the floor.

He passed through a door into a small office. It had a

desk and a computer terminal and a filing cabinet in it, and a green carpet on the floor. Beyond was a glass door reading TO THE ELEVATORS. He sighed in relief.

But on the other side of the door was a little office with a desk and a computer terminal and a filing cabinet and a green carpet, and a glass door reading TO THE ELEVATORS. And after that, another. It was a long series of offices, one after the other.

He was in the fifth little office when he began noticing a funny smell. He was in the seventh little office when he noticed something oozing out of the ventilator duct. It was a pale yellow something. It was steaming. By the ninth little office with TO THE ELEVATORS on the door he was getting really scared.

The ooze was flowing onto the carpet. He poked it with his shoe; then, when that seemed safe, he dipped his finger in it and sniffed.

"Cheese."

Hot cheese. Molten. Mozzarella, like on pizzas. Only this was on pale green carpet, flowing. He hurried.

Flaming apes, Lord Gomztooth had said. Nothing about molten cheese.

By the nineteenth little room with a terminal and a filing cabinet, he was slipping and sliding through steaming floods of cheese. He groped over cheese-covered chairs and desks.

The twentieth door marked TO THE ELEVATORS opened into a great room that stretched as far as he could see, with desks bearing telephones on them every few meters. The room was ankle-deep in hot cheese. And filling.

He started off in the most promising direction, slopping through the mess. He fell down twice and got covered with steamy warm strands of cheese. When it reached the level of the chairs, red lights began flashing around the walls, and a mechanical voice sounded.

"Peligro! Queso caliente de Martes!"

The alarm went off every thirty seconds. He struggled to a desktop and tried a telephone. The only reply he could get was, *"Queso caliente de Martes!"*

He began jumping from desktop to desktop. If the cheese got any higher, he'd have to swim in it. He sure wished the cheese was flaming apes.

Panic was just about to set in when he heard a voice.

"Hello! Over there!"

It was coming from the deep darkness at the end of the

room. Ralph could dimly see a figure in some sort of boat floating amid the desks and wisps of steam.

Ralph began jumping up and down and yelling. But the cheese was all over and his foot slipped in it. Right off the desk he tumbled and *glub!* into the hot cheese. He thrashed to the top and started swimming toward the boat. The cheese wasn't really hard to swim through. Just disgusting.

Finally he was close enough to see his rescuer, a gangly young man with black frizzy hair and a mustache. He was wearing sort of old-fashioned clothes. There was an I'VE BEEN TO HOLE CONTROL balloon tied to his belt. The guy extended an oar to Ralph and he hauled himself on board, trailing strands of cheese. He sprawled on the bottom of the black boat, gasping.

"A lucky thing I was here," the man said. "You were in trouble." He had some kind of foreign accent.

"Y-yeah. It was getting close. Where is all that cheese coming from, anyway?" Ralph wondered aloud, picking strings of cheese from his clothes.

"Mars, I think. Didn't you hear the warning announcement? It was in Spanish, and it said, 'Warning! Hot cheese from Mars!'"

"Oh. Is *that* what that was? I don't speak Spanish. Cheese from Mars, huh?"

"Yes. Didn't Lord Gomztooth tell you about the cheese? But then, I guess he wouldn't have if he didn't give you a hole like this."

Ralph noticed that he wasn't floating in a boat as he had first thought. It was a big, dry hole with equations and numbers doodled all over it. The cheese just sort of rolled up to it and stopped.

"We're in a hole!" Ralph shouted.

"Yes, we are. Didn't Lord Gomztooth tell you anything about space really being formed from Swiss cheese, and this place being one of the holes in it? Didn't he tell you about hole mechanics?"

Ralph shook his head. He took a look at the guy's map, which was spread on the bottom of the hole. It was totally different from his, but in this place that hardly mattered.

"No," Ralph explained as they rowed, "he only told me about the flaming apes, and gave me this umbrella for protection. Are you on your way to the roof too?"

"Flaming apes! Yes, I am on my way to the roof. What is your name, young fellow?"

"Ralph. Ralph Fozbek. What's yours?"

"Albert. Albert Einstein."

Suddenly Ralph recognized the frizzy hair and the little mustache. It *was* Einstein! Only he was young—he looked like a teenager.

"What are you doing here?" Ralph gulped.

"Trying to get out, my boy." Einstein pulled his oar noisily out of the cheese.

7: Founder's Day

"BUT . . . you're famous!"

Einstein shook his head. "But I am only a patent clerk, working on a few mathematical theories when I can find the time."

"Yeah, but later you got famous. After it turned out you were right. You even predicted the atomic . . ."

Ralph suddenly realized what he was saying. This Einstein was from the past—sometime in the early 1900s. If Ralph told him all about what happened later, he might alter history.

"The atomic what?" Einstein said as he lit up his pipe.

"The . . . the atomic stopwatch. Yeah. You predicted a lot of other stuff too."

"Then I take it you are from . . ."

"The future, yeah, that's right." As briefly as he could, Ralph told Einstein the story of how he came to be floating in a lake of cheese in the center of a black hole. He went around all the parts he thought could change history.

Then it was Einstein's turn.

He had been trapped in the hole for hours and hours, it turned out. He had been working on a theory during his coffee break at the patent office he worked in. The year was 1904. He was imagining himself traveling the speed of light, wondering how that would affect the flow of time. Then he had become very drowsy, and had fallen asleep on his Swiss cheese sandwich. When he awakened, he found himself sitting on the sofa in Lord Gomztooth's waiting room with the sandwich stuck to his forehead. He was number MC^2, and there was an armadillo next to him reading a magazine.

"And that is how I found myself in this predicament," he explained. "Lord Gomztooth told me I could get out if I traveled to the roof and completed my theory before Founder's Day. I have been working on it, as you see."

Ralph glanced at the scribbles all over the hole. "But how could you travel here without an H32 helmet? This is a black hole. The gravity here is so strong not even light can escape."

Einstein shrugged. "It was a thought experiment. Perhaps my thought protects me. Gravity, you say, affects *light* here?

Fascinating." He erased part of his figuring with his sleeve, and wrote some more.

Ralph took over paddling the hole while Einstein continued his equations, mumbling in German. The large pair of doors at the opposite end of the big room looked like the right direction in which to head. It was easy to push through the cheese. The flood seemed to have stopped just above the level of the desks. It was like a big yellow pond.

Just as they reached the doors, a clock appeared, floating over them like a blue bubble.

"Fifteen minutes to Founder's Day," it announced.

Ralph had almost forgotten. Lord Gomztooth had said something about everything shutting down in forty-five minutes.

He had to hurry.

The latch to the doors was below cheese level, and Ralph had to reach deep into the warm sticky stuff to find it. Finally the doors sprang open. There was no cheese beyond, and they were carried down into a hallway by a yellow surge as the room emptied. The floating blue clock followed them.

When the cheese thinned out enough, they rolled up the hole and slurped through the revolving door at the end of the hall. Little of the cheese got through with them, except for clinging strands.

"It looks like some sort of lobby," Einstein said, pointing with his pipe.

The room was really big, with potted plants and marble columns. Ralph found the light switch behind a velvet curtain. Einstein's map indicated they should go around to the left.

"Thirteen minutes to Founder's Day," the clock said.

"We'd better hurry," Ralph said, and began walking as fast as he could. "What do you think this Founder's Day really is, Mr. Einstein?"

"Well, it could possibly indicate—"

There was a horrible screeching noise above them. They both dove for cover behind a potted palm. A big sheet of flame smacked into the tile floor. It was shaped like a chimpanzee.

"Here come the flaming apes," Ralph shouted.

"Flaming apes!" Einstein muttered as he rolled up his hole.

Ralph opened his umbrella just as two more plunged screaming from the ceiling. They looked like howler monkeys. They certainly sounded like them. They disappeared into the black dome of the umbrella as if they had somehow fallen through it, but did not come out the underside.

"Remarkable," Einstein remarked. "They appear to be materializing, or perhaps entering this dimension, just below the ceiling. They are falling nearly the speed of sound, and are burning up in the atmosphere. It makes one think that if—"

"Think later," Ralph yelled, and made a run for it just as two more hit the floor in a shower of sparks.

Einstein caught up with him. More apes were falling. Sparks were everywhere, like fireflies. Apes were screaming at the speed of sound, smashing into potted plants and sofas. Most of the apes were sopranos. It sounded just like the opera. Monkeys flashed by them, burning baboons, infernos of orangutans. There was even a huge roaring gorilla, who burned out before landing like a meteor.

"Ten minutes to Founder's Day," the floating clock intoned. Ralph took a swipe at it with the umbrella, but it kept following them.

The ape drizzle increased to a shower. Everything was ablaze, but all Ralph and Einstein had to do was dodge ape craters and keep under the umbrella. The funny thing was, when an ape would land on the umbrella, there was no recoil. It didn't even jar. It was a hole with a handle. As he ran Ralph tried not to wonder where the apes were falling to.

They had almost reached the end of the room when the rain began slowing. A couple of howling gibbons smashed through a model of a building in a glass booth, and they were the last. But Ralph and Einstein stood under the umbrella as they walked, just the same.

"I guess it's over," Ralph finally said, and folded the umbrella.

Then he realized they were standing next to a brass pole which disappeared into a deep hole in the floor.

"Not again," Ralph whimpered.

"According to my map," Einstein said, "this should be the way to the elevators."

"Great," Ralph said.

"Eight minutes to Founder's Day," the clock said.

"I shall practice my thought experiment about the speed of light during the journey," Einstein muttered to himself. He vanished down the pole.

Ralph took a big breath and jumped. It was a rerun of the first pole, only faster, if possible. Again the floors

whipped by. He closed his eyes. At last he began slowing. His stomach caught up with him by the time he had landed firmly on the floor. He opened his eyes.

There were four elevators in front of him. They looked awfully familiar. The floor in front of them was a bright tile mosaic of the Marx Brothers. Then he looked up at the ceiling, where the brass pole disappeared into a long trench. He gulped. There was an escalator up there.

It was where he had been standing before, when he took the first brass pole trip. It was the same brass pole! He had traveled it now in two different directions. He had slid up it before, and now down it. Gravity had changed directions somewhere inside the hole. He decided not to mention that.

"Phenomenal journey," Einstein said to himself, and punched the elevator button.

The doors opened, and they stepped inside. "Where do you want to go, sir or madam?" the elevator said.

"The roof," Ralph responded.

"This dimension, please," Einstein added thoughtfully.

In no time at all the doors opened again. The roof stretched as far as they could see on any side. It was dark, with no stars at all. They stepped off the elevator. As a matter of fact, it was *too* dark. It was like being inside a black velvet bag.

"Here it is," Einstein said.

There was a shed beside the elevator marked FUSES, CRYSTAL BROOMS, SANDWICHES. But there was a huge padlock on the door. It was the biggest padlock Ralph had ever seen.

"Oh, no! What are we going to do now?"

"Five minutes to Founder's Day," the clock droned.

Ralph took another swipe at it with the umbrella. He looked right at it, for the first time. He noticed something.

"Hey, this clock is backwards!" The 1 was where the 11 should have been.

"Hmmmmm . . . yes," Einstein said. "Backwards."

Then they both began studying the lock. It took only a moment for them to glance at each other, then back at the clock suspiciously.

"You don't suppose . . . ?" Ralph began.

"Backwards. Yes. If this place is indeed moving as fast as you said, that might just make time flow in reverse . . . according to my new theory, of course."

"Backwards in time? Hey, maybe that's why the hole picked you up too."

"Perhaps that explains also the mystery of Founder's Day. In five minutes this place will arrive at the moment it was created. If it doesn't stop, everything here will become . . . uncreated."

"The big bang*," Ralph muttered in awe.

"The what?"

"The big explosion that started everything! That's where we're headed!"

"Interesting concept."

"Maybe, but I don't want to see it up close!" Ralph yelled as he attacked the padlock.

Einstein began helping him attack it. They tried pulling it off, and hammered it with their shoes. Frantically they searched for door hinges but couldn't find any.

*See Krebnickel's Glossary

"Four minutes to Founder's Day."

Ralph was attempting to chew the lock off when he noticed Einstein had stopped helping and was just sitting there. Ralph screamed at him.

Einstein replied calmly, "Sometimes, if you just sit down and stop trying so hard, the answer will come to you. It works with equations."

Ralph couldn't believe it. Just minutes to the end of everything, and here was this guy just sitting there! He was as much of a nerd as Louie! Ralph lost his temper and tried clobbering Einstein with his umbrella. But the scientist ducked and the umbrella just grazed the rolled-up hole stuck in his belt. The collision produced blue sparks that floated away and faded. Ralph was about to strike again when he noticed the expression on Einstein's face.

"Electrons*! That's it!" He jumped up and unfolded his hole. Then he spread it evenly over the front of the shed. It was big and black.

"I'm not going through there!" Ralph said. "What happened to those apes? That hole goes into some other dimension."

"Three minutes to Founder's Day."

"Just give me your umbrella!"

Ralph did. Einstein opened it and pushed it slowly into the larger hole. The blue sparks happened again, a lot of them. Then they stopped and the umbrella resisted his push. The handle snapped to attention. Einstein couldn't move it. And then, through the space where the umbrella was sup-

*See Krebnickel's Glossary

posed to be, they could see inside the shed.

"It's a hole in a hole," Ralph said dizzily.

They could just squeeze into the shed around the umbrella handle. Once inside, they turned on the lights. The shed was filled with switch boxes and vending machines and big quartz crystals. Beside the storage area was the elevator shaft and all its cables. When they turned around, they could see the roof and sky through the hole. The umbrella handle appeared to be stuck in midair.

After a short search, they located the fuse box for Quadrant 7. It was yellow. Ralph pulled the switch.

They looked at each other. Nothing felt different at all. There was no sound, no spark.

"Ah," said Einstein. "Perhaps we are only halfway there. You have done your part. But perhaps *both* Earthlings must finish their tasks. You have thrown the switch, as Lord Gomztooth suggested. But he told *me* that I must finish my formula. I will work on that."

"Two minutes to Founder's Day."

Ralph freaked out and started pulling switches, yelling about the big bang. Einstein grabbed his arm when he picked up a quartz crystal and tried to beat open a circuit-box door. Einstein was yelling in German.

There was so much noise that they never heard the racket of the sales force climbing up the elevator shaft. When the robots clambered into the shed, Ralph and Einstein were still struggling over the crystal.

"Hi, there, fella," the first robot said. It extended its shiny pink hand.

They stopped struggling.

More robots were coming, hauling themselves up the elevator cables, grinning. Their hair was perfect. Their burgundy suits swished.

"Hello. The name's Bob," they all said. "We're looking for a Ralph."

Einstein said something in German.

"Ah," the Bobs said. "Ralph. We're from the Hole Control Mutual Equation Club. Our records show you passed through our showroom without giving us the chance to tell you how our policy can save you a great deal of trouble."

"What?" Einstein said.

"Why, of course I could give you a sample!" the Bobs said, winking. "For a minimal fee, you understand. Have you got a Swiss cheese sandwich on you, by any chance? Ah, good."

Einstein's eyes had glazed over as the sales robots were talking to him. "Don't listen to them!" Ralph screamed. He had seen the same look on his father's face when the encyclopedia man had sold him all those mining books.

"One minute to Founder's Day."

It was too late! Einstein muttered something and pulled the sandwich out of his pocket. Before Ralph could stop him, the deal was made.

"Congratulations!" the first Bob said, stuffing the sandwich into a briefcase strapped to his back. "The Hole Control retail team is glad to offer you a sample of what could be yours if you decide to enroll in the full Enlightenment in Physics course."

A second robot stepped closer. "First, learn about the surprising dimensions of time. What a can of wormholes! For instance, imagine that you have gone so fast that time is actually flowing backwards. What would *you* do? Well, statistics show that if you just turn to the left and give the hands on that big blue clock a stern push in the right direction, everything will flow back to normal."

"That's right," another Bob said. "And don't forget, $E = mc^2$, Ralph."

Einstein's jaw dropped. His pipe fell out. "Of course!"

Ralph dove for the clock. He shoved its hands. There was a moment when his stomach felt like a big, fast elevator was stopping, only the elevator was moving through time. His stomach fluttered. Then the clock disappeared. There was a crackle and surging sound from the Quadrant 7 fuse box.

"We did it!" Ralph shouted. "We turned the flow of time back around!"

"$E = mc^2$," Einstein repeated dazedly.

"Now Dr. Krebnickel's neutrino turbine will work! Louie'll never believe how we did it."

"$E = mc^2$. Of course." Einstein blinked.

"That's right," the Bobs said. "These and many other mysteries can be opened to you when you sign up for the full Enlightenment in Physics course."

"How much does it cost?" Einstein said.

"Forty-seven pounds of cheese," the lead Bob replied. "Just sign right here."

A paper unfolded in front of Einstein, who immediately signed it in chalk.

The Bobs slapped each other on the back, assured Einstein, whom they still called Ralph, that he would never be sorry, and climbed back down the elevator shaft.

"Boy, *I* was worried about giving too much away. They told him the big formula," Ralph muttered to himself as he squeezed through the umbrella hole.

Einstein held the elevator door open for him, but Ralph explained that all he had to do was turn the dial on his H32 helmet back to zero to return to Earth.

"Very well. That's very convenient. I, on the other hand, must travel back through this very odd building. It has been an enlightening meeting, Ralph. I'd shake your hand, only I'm afraid it might affect space-time."

Ralph laughed. "Thanks for the offer. It was really great

meeting you, Albert. You've got a great life ahead of you."

Einstein chuckled and shrugged.

Ralph took one last look at Einstein and turned his helmet dial back to zero. He waved good-bye as he faded.

8 : Lieutenant Duckworth

BBBBBBBBZZZZZZZZZZZIIIIIIIIIIIINNNNNNN
NNGGGGGGGGG!!!

He took the same sickening elevator ride back to ordinary space-time. At the end all his molecules shook, like a very old car trying to go too fast.

POP!

He skidded into reality in a shower of blue electrons.

Dr. Krebnickel peered at him with wide eyes.

"Are you all right, my boy?"

"Ralph! What happened?" Louie shouted.

He was back in the laboratory. And in the background the neutrino turbine hummed.

"It worked!" Ralph yelled. "We did fix it!"

"It appears you did. But you should never have tried such a reckless thing," Dr. Krebnickel chided. Ralph sagged onto a crate and glared at Louie.

"It wasn't *my* idea, Professor."

"What's that balloon for?" Louie said. "And why do you smell like pizza?"

"Now, now, just a moment," Dr. Krebnickel interrupted. "Let's give him a chance to breathe."

Dr. Krebnickel brought some tea, and after a few sips Ralph began to feel more normal. He tried to untie the balloon from his belt, but all that did was shake out some holes from his pocket. Four or five of them, of different sizes. They fluttered out onto the floor, where they became pits. Dr. Krebnickel was excited, and measured them.

"I must have picked them up in the Hole Press Room. How long have I been gone?" Ralph asked.

"Only about ten minutes," Louie responded.

"Wow. I was in that place for hours!"

"Ya. But you were traveling so fast time was compressed!" Dr. Krebnickel explained as he helped Ralph out of the H32 helmet. Ralph's hair was all sweaty and stuck to his head.

Ralph shook his hair out, then noticed the expression on Louie's face. "What's wrong?"

"Your hair, Ralph, it's . . . it's purple!"

A limp strand fell in front of his eyes. Louie was right. It looked like grape bubble gum. Ralph freaked out.

"I'm going to tell them you did it, Louie! When my mother sees this, I'm going to tell her you gave me drugs that turned my hair purple! My dad will kill you! I nearly got killed by flaming apes because of you. And now . . . now I'm a punk! Are my ears pierced too? Any tattoos?"

Dr. Krebnickel jumped between the two of them and motioned down Ralph's swinging arms. "Now, now. I'm sure Quarwyn and I can work out a formula later that will bring your hair back to normal. But it would help if you told us exactly what happened."

Ralph gradually calmed down. He had some more tea.

He told the whole story, first in dribs and drabs, and then in floods: the cheese, Einstein, the flaming apes, everything.

"Purple lizards?" Louie sputtered. "Sales robots? The big bang? But . . . why . . . what . . . who . . . ?"

Louie was overloading. Dr. Krebnickel had to hold him down and stuff a test-tube warmer in his mouth so Ralph could finish.

Louie stopped struggling when Ralph got to the part about Einstein getting the equation from the robot Bob. He just gurgled.

"So," Dr. Krebnickel wondered, "that is how my old friend Albert did it. He got his famous formula from a black hole."

"Yeah," Ralph said. "It's the truth."

Dr. Krebnickel slapped Ralph on the back. Louie tried to. They all stood around the happily whirring turbine and just smiled wearily. The hole was back in its pickle jar, in its proper space-time. Dr. Krebnickel would get his contract with the power company. Everything was going to be okay.

"Hey," Louie said. "We've got to get this thing ready for the power authority. First, we roll it up the loading ramp at the back of the lab . . ."

"Oh, come on." Ralph moaned. "I'm exhausted!"

"I'm afraid he's right, Ralph. I know it's late, and you're welcome to go home, but I have to load the turbine into the truck. It will take hours."

"Home?" Ralph repeated weakly. "Bed? Sleep?" Just the words made him dreamy.

"Oh, don't be silly," Louie said as he began hoisting one side of the turbine with an old jack. "He's just kidding, Doc. Ralph will stay and help. Won't you, Ralph?"

Something happened then that saved Loony Louie's life. Ralph was on top of him, trying to find his throat. Suddenly a loud humming sound overtook the humming of the turbine. Jars and instruments rattled. The laboratory was flooded with purple light.

"Peligro! Peligro!" said a loud mechanical voice.

Ralph gulped. The voice sounded terribly familiar.

A large tunnel appeared in some shelves across the room. It was velvety black, and circular. A big shiny motorcycle rumbled out with a lavender patrolman on it. He stopped, stepped off, shook his long tail, and pushed up his goggles. He had all sorts of chrome badges and buckles on his leather jacket.

He blinked at Ralph with bright green eyes and saluted. "Lieutenant Duckworth, of the Hole Control Patrol, sir. Took me a while to find you. Didn't know you people lived underground." Lieutenant Duckworth grinned. He had bright yellow teeth.

"It was *true!*" Louie squeaked. "I didn't really believe all that stuff."

"Amazing," said the professor, peering at the hole in the wall.

"W-what do you want?" Ralph gulped.

"I am here to give you a ticket," the lavender cop said, flipping open a book. "A citation. You entered Hole Control without a license, young man."

Ralph blinked. "Great! Just great! I risk my life to start the professor's black hole up, go all the way to the beginning of the universe and back again, and what thanks do I get? A traffic ticket!"

"Yeah! That's not fair!" Louie yelled, to Ralph's surprise.

"Just a moment," Dr. Krebnickel said. "Isn't there some way we can deal with this other than a ticket? Ralph was only trying to help me. Couldn't you give him the license exam instead?"

"Oh," Lieutenant Duckworth said. "Well, you see, I'm not authorized to make any decisions on this trip. Just deliver the ticket. Now your full name, please . . ."

Ralph pretended he was his father and the lieutenant was a pestering insurance salesman. He gave him the Fozbek Look.

Lieutenant Duckworth became distressed and began shifting from foot to foot. "Please, sir, I am not empowered to make any decisions whatsoever on this trip."

"You're not making any," Ralph bellowed, "I am. I have decided you're going to give me a license instead of a ticket."

Lieutenant Duckworth looked puzzled for a moment, then shrugged. "Lord Gomztooth never said anything about someone else making decisions. I guess you're right, sir."

"I am? I mean, now you're talking!"

While Lieutenant Duckworth got the license exam out of his motorcycle, Dr. Krebnickel whispered to Ralph, "Don't worry. It's easy. I've had my license for years. Just remember to think of the color purple, and you'll do fine."

Ralph thought of the scores on his fifth-grade finals. "Well, maybe I should study a little first . . ."

"I MUST CONDUCT THIS TEST!" Lieutenant Duckworth exploded. "Not another decision until you answer the questions!"

"Uh, okay. Sorry."

"First question: When entering hyperspace, should you signal by touching your nose or by extending your left arm?"

Ralph gulped. He thought purple. "By extending your arm?"

"Right. Next question: Who is the greatest batter of all time?"

"Hank Aaron." Ralph grinned.

"Next question: Why is the sky dark at night?"

"Because it's hard to sleep with the light on?"

"Right. Which of the following is the correct meaning of *Cosa Nostra?* A. A small village in Sicily. B. The nose curse of the Andes. C. BankAmericard."

Think purple. Purple. "A," he said.

"Next question . . ."

Nobody heard the next question, because at that point the neutrino turbine stopped whining. A lot of silence happened, and they all turned around. There was no pickle jar in the turbine, none at all!

"Look, Professor, it's floating!" Louie yelled.

There was the pickle jar with the black hole in it, bobbing around about six feet from the floor, making its way toward the hole in the ceiling. Floating! Just like the H32 helmet had in Ralph's room.

"Not again!" Dr. Krebnickel shrieked. "It's Heminglas, and his infernal gravity machine!" He made a lunge and just managed to grab the jar as it floated over the chemistry table. It sank down for a second with his weight, then bobbed up with Dr. Krebnickel hanging on to it. Ralph and Louie wrapped around the professor's feet, but only ended up on the floor clutching a blue suede loafer each. Dr. Krebnickel floated up and out through the hole in the ceiling. His plaid socks disappeared last.

"Take care of Quarwyn, boys!" he managed to howl. "I'll get back somehow!"

A piece of glass fell and broke. In all the silence it made a terrible racket. Ralph and Louie looked at each other hopelessly.

Lieutenant Duckworth cleared his throat. "Interesting habits you humans have. Now, next question—"

"What are you talking about?" Ralph shrieked. It was real late. He had been to a black hole, and Dr. Krebnickel had just floated through his roof under the power of Dr. Heminglas. Now this purple lizard was trying to give him a test.

"Yeah," Louie yelled. *"you're a cop*. Do something about this. Dr. Krebnickel has been kidnapped!"

Lieutenant Duckworth blinked. He looked like he was trying very hard to think. "I have no authority to make decisions, sir. I would like to help you, but I am only here to give you the examination. But this does seem to be an interference with the legal processes of the Hole Control, and I will call my superiors for advice."

"You're no help."

"Wait, Ralph, look! The gravity gauge."

Louie's strange invention was working. The needle was pointing wildly toward Teehalt Park.

"C'mon, let's follow it," Louie said.

Ralph watched Louie clamber up the table and out the window. He wished he would suddenly be so tired he would faint. But he didn't, so he figured he had to follow Louie.

He tore a big hole in his shirt as he wiggled out the window.

Lieutenant Duckworth was unsure what he should do. He consulted his big blue watch, which was floating over the holecycle. Then he thought for a while, hoping to come upon some plan without making a decision. But that was hard to do. At last he cranked up the tachyphone and tried to call home. That didn't work either. There was some powerful gravitational device about that was making awful static.

The laboratory was very quiet. Lieutenant Duckworth was worried. Going home involved making a decision too. He flapped his arms in frustration and made the holese frustration noise. A faraway duck answered him.

Then he noticed the electrical cord leading to Quarwyn, and the plug on the floor where it had fallen from the wall.

He made the frustration noise again. This time the duck fluttered down through the hole in Dr. Krebnickel's house and landed on the lieutenant's shoulder. The duck made soft quacks and snuggled closer.

9 : Mount Hortense

WHEN Ralph and Louie got outside, they found a huge balloon high over Dr. Krebnickel's oak tree. It was a Jules Verne kind of balloon, with a basket, but it had antennas and disks all over it, and some kind of rocket motor. Dr. Krebnickel was floating up toward the balloon, kicking. Ralph and Louie could hear wicked laughter coming from the basket, and flashes of electricity.

"It's Heminglas!" Louie gasped.

They watched helplessly as the balloon, followed by the squirming shadow of Dr. Krebnickel, disappeared over the trees.

"What do we do now?" Louie whined.

"Let's go to sleep," Ralph said.

Ralph didn't mean it, but Louie wasn't listening anyway. He ducked into the laboratory window, and was back in a moment with his gravity gauge and the H32 helmet. Groggily Ralph watched him wire it to the handlebars of his bicycle.

"What are you doing?" he mumbled.

"Here, put this on," Louie said, shoving the helmet his way.

Before he knew it, Ralph was sitting on the front handlebars of the bike wearing the helmet, the gravity gauge between his knees. Louie stuck a piece of wire in front of his face.

"If I'm right, we can cause a huge gravity field to form between the helmet and the black hole. Here, bite this."

Ralph opened his mouth to protest, and Louie stuck the wire in it. The bicycle started glowing. The gravity gauge started singing. It *sounded* like singing anyway, sort of like the operas Ralph's mother liked to listen to.

"It's working," Louie bubbled excitedly. "Hold on."

Louie punched a button and, with a jolt, the bicycle started rolling. The gauge sang higher. The bicycle bounced down the hill past Dr. Krebnickel's house and skidded into the road. It picked up speed, jumped the curb, and began traveling cross-country through Teehalt Park. They went over a little bridge and headed into the playground. The balloon tied to him beat an annoying rhythm on his H32 helmet.

"Heeeeeeaa. Stpppp goaaanng ssssss fasssst," Ralph said around the wire.

"Oh, that's not me," Louie said. "My feet are not even on the pedals. The gravity gauge is being pulled by an attraction to Dr. Heminglas's machinery."

A swing set loomed. Ralph screamed.

The bike swerved when he did that, and he found that he could control its path by biting the wire. Bite on the left, swerve to the right, and vice versa. He bit really hard and just missed one of the giant concrete frogs that littered the playground.

The trip through Teehalt Park was a nightmare. Ralph *wished* it were a nightmare. That way, at least he would be dreaming. Finally the bike jumped back onto a street and they were in the open. They swooped up a long ramp and ended up on the expressway, going faster and faster. Ralph wanted to ask Louie why they were no longer headed toward Dr. Heminglas's mansion, but he was afraid to let go of the wire. The balloon was getting smaller and smaller against the clouds. Ralph couldn't see Dr. Krebnickel at all anymore.

The expressway flashed by in a blur now, and they passed the few cars they saw in just a few seconds. The faces of the people in them were full of surprise.

They just zipped faster and faster, heading out of the city. For nearly an hour they traveled through the darkness. The road got hillier and hillier, until Ralph realized they were headed into the Lugo Mountains. They were real craggy mountains, and the interstate wound around and around through their peaks. Ralph closed his eyes the last twenty miles, right after the first sharp curves started. Louie had to shout out instructions.

Then the bicycle jumped the curb again, and went right up the mountainside. Ralph knew this because of the vibration—his eyes were still closed. Grass rustled beneath them and pulled at the tires. Fir trees whipped by. Ralph couldn't hear Louie's yelled instructions anymore.

But when he heard Louie scream he opened his eyes.

There was a wall right in front of them, with the balloon towering on the other side.

BAM!

You really do see stars when you get knocked out. That made a big impression on Ralph. So did the wall.

He woke up with the wire stuck between his teeth like dental floss. Around him were a lot of electronic instruments. The Hole Control balloon bobbed, still stubbornly tethered to his belt. Bright lights lined the ceiling. He blinked up at a fat man wearing a loud checkered suit, with a cigarette in a long holder in his mouth.

"Dr. Heminglas!"

"Hello, my boy. My very clever little purple-haired boy."

"Oh, he's not the clever one," Ralph heard Louie say. "He just steered. I fixed up the gravity gauge and everything."

Dr. Heminglas's eyes narrowed.

"Shut up, brat!"

Somehow, it made Ralph feel better about Dr. Heminglas that he couldn't stand Louie either. Then he remembered the stolen hole. He tried to kick Dr. Heminglas, but found that his arms and legs were tied. He slid off the table and plunked onto the floor, which reminded him of being knocked out, because he saw stars again. Through the stars he could see Louie and Dr. Krebnickel all tied up too.

"Ow! Hey, where are we?"

"Somewhere in the Lugo Mountains," Dr. Krebnickel said. "I saw that much before we came down."

Dr. Heminglas smiled widely. He gestured around them at the gigantic laboratory they were in. Computers ringed the walls, blinking and clicking. Tubes gurgled with strange liquids. Cookie jars bulged with junk food, and there were several Twinkie machines beside the computers.

"We are in my secret laboratory," Dr. Heminglas hissed. "Deep within my private peak: Mount Hortense, named for my mother. We're in the center of solid granite. No instrument can possibly locate you now. No one knows I have an actual black hole." He held up the purple-black pickle jar and gazed lovingly at it.

Ralph thought of Hole Control, deep inside that jar. Lord Gomztooth, and the Bobs. All those lavender secretaries. They were all in the hands of a madman. It made him really angry. He wriggled in his ropes. Being dopey from staying up all night, dizzy from running into the wall, and angry, too, was a heady combination.

"You stole that hole!" Dr. Krebnickel shouted. "Just like you stole the formula for my wart remover, and the atomic necktie, and . . ."

"Please." Dr. Heminglas chuckled. "Do not waste such

moral preaching on me, Ladislav. I have made a fortune without such silly concepts. You can't pin me down with them now."

"What are you going to do with that hole?" Dr. Krebnickel insisted.

"Ahhhhhh, Heminglas muttered to himself. "First I shall take certain measurements, and my computer shall record everything about it. Then I shall make a phone call to some friends of mine who would be very interested in laying hands on such a find."

"The Russians!" Dr. Krebnickel said.

"How did you know that?" Heminglas snapped.

"Statistics! There are no warts in the Soviet Union! That's where you sold my wart remover, you beast!"

"Ha! Beast, eh? Perhaps my friends would also be interested in a washed-up old scientist and his assistants. I will see if I can get an extra million for you, Ladislav."

"You can't do that!" Ralph yelled.

Dr. Heminglas laughed. "There is nothing to stop me, young fellow. Not even Dr. Krebnickel's famous computer could find you here. And nothing can get through these walls."

"He's right, Ralph," Louie piped in. "That much granite can block everything except neutrinos."

Ralph glared at Louie. "Ha! That shows how much you know! Granite can't stop Lieutenant Duckworth of the Hole Control Patrol! He's probably on his way here right now!"

"What are you talking about?" Dr. Heminglas said, glancing nervously around.

"I bet he is!" Ralph yelled, a little too hysterically. "I bet he's coming to arrest you, with handcuffs made out of Swiss cheese!"

Dr. Heminglas grinned. "That was a nasty blow on the head, wasn't it? Obviously you're delirious, poor boy."

"Are you okay, Ralph?" Louie said. "That guy'll never make a decision."

Ralph gave Louie a really poisonous look. He hoped there was no antidote.

"Bring me the telephone, B-12," Dr. Heminglas exclaimed to someone over his shoulder. "An overseas line, please."

A wiry robot wheeled into the room. It was connected by a jointed arm to tracks in the ceiling. It offered Dr. Heminglas a red phone. "Yes, sir," it said.

Dr. Heminglas spoke a number into the phone.

"My. Do I need oiling?" the robot asked.

"What? No, of course not, fool. Yes, hello, Operator?"

"Then what is that noise?" the robot continued while Dr. Heminglas spoke. "Do you not hear it, sir?"

"Who, me?" Ralph said.

"He's right," said Louie. "Listen. It's . . . it's . . ."

"It's a siren!" Dr. Krebnickel sat up.

Suddenly the mountain began shaking. It seemed like a very familiar shaking to Ralph. The room filled with purple light.

"Earthquake!" Dr. Heminglas squealed.

"Peligro! Peligro!"

Ralph whooped as the big tunnel appeared in the wall.

Lieutenant Duckworth was really on his way!

Dr. Heminglas turned real pale, and dropped the phone. But he quickly gathered his wits again. He hustled all of them into a garage, huffing and puffing, and crammed them into the backseat of his limousine. A series of granite doors opened, and the car peeled out of a long driveway onto the winding mountain road, tires screeching.

"Whoever that is will never catch me now," he panted. "You are a great deal of trouble to me, Krebnickel. But I shall make enough off you to make up for it."

"No, you won't," Ralph yelled. "Because that's Lieutenant Duckworth back there. He's the most feared cop in the Hole Control Patrol. When he catches up with you you won't be making any deals."

"What? Hole Control Patrol?"

"Yeah. What a mean bunch! Dr. Krebnickel has to pay them thousands a month just to leave him in one piece. You didn't think he was really that poor, did you? He had to pay for that hole! And no one can move it unless Duckworth says it's okay!"

The siren noise crept up behind them until it was a shrill warble. Dr. Heminglas cursed. Ralph wriggled up and looked out the back window. It was Lieutenant Duckworth, right behind them, with his chrome zippers flying, goggles down.

The prisoners cheered.

Dr. Heminglas growled, and pressed his foot to the floor. Lieutenant Duckworth turned on two rotating purple lights on his cycle. But he was having a hard time keeping up with the speeding car. He made some kind of call on his cycle radio. The car screeched around a sharp bend, and when Ralph next saw the lieutenant he had a plastic gun in his hand. Dr. Heminglas took a gun out of his glove compartment and fired out the window at him.

Lieutenant Duckworth, erect and noble as a Mountie, raised his pistol and fired. It made a firecracker noise, and a yellow flash shot over the car and hit the roof. It was a huge gob of hot cheese! Strings of mozzarella fluttered in the wind. More shots were exchanged, and soon the whole car looked like a flying pizza. Dr. Heminglas swerved along trying to see between the strands of steaming cheese.

But the pops were getting further and further away as Dr. Heminglas accelerated to top speed. Between the globs of cheese Ralph could see the lieutenant diminishing behind them.

"Ha. I've lost him. And I'm not even at top speed!" Heminglas bragged. "Some hotshot outfit, this Hole Patrol."

Suddenly, above them there was a loud helicopter noise. Something like a big black shadow fluttered down beside the car, like a pancake falling.

"What was that?" Heminglas shouted. He was getting really freaked. Ralph's story was getting to him.

Another one flapped down outside. It landed on the mountain and formed a big black crater. Ralph looked up to see Lieutenant Duckworth, his cycle transformed into a helicopter, following close overhead. He fired his gun, and a black shadow fluttered by the car. Heminglas swerved.

"They're holes!" Ralph yelled. "He's shooting holes at us! Ha, you're done now, Heminglas!"

Then another one fell a good hundred yards from them, squarely on the road. It was a big black hole across both lanes. Dr. Heminglas, eyes bugged out, clenched on brakes.

The car squealed sideways and fell *whump!* into the hole. It was not a sudden jar, but a bump and then a slow sinking sensation. It was as black as night inside. Dr. Heminglas, howling, opened his door, and a thick wall of hot cheese oozed in. He slipped and slid in it, making horrible growling noises.

Ralph managed to slip his hands around his tied feet, and then it was simple to untie himself and the other two. They clambered over Dr. Heminglas and onto the roof of the car. It was slowly sinking in a hole full of hot cheese. Ralph jumped for the edge of the hole and got his hands on pavement. From there he could pull Louie and the professor up.

The Hole Control Patrol copter was circling above them. It's rotor was a big spinning black hole. Lieutenant Duckworth set the machine down and quickly converted it back into a motorcycle. He got off and took out his pad.

"Now. Next question: What color is the sky on Mars?"

Ralph laughed. "Pink. You're a very persistent guy, Lieutenant Duckworth."

"One must accomplish one's mission, mustn't one, sir? That concludes your examination. Thank you for your cooperation. I am authorized by the Galactic Hole Control to present you with this learner's permit." He handed Ralph a plastic card.

"You mean he passed the test?" Louie said in amazement.

"Yes, sir. You see, it doesn't matter how you answer the questions as long as you take the test."

"And the only reason you rescued us was to finish that test?"

"I have my orders, sir."

They were interrupted by noises from the hole. Dr. Heminglas was clambering around on the sticky roof of his car, trying to jump to the edge, and falling down a lot. Ralph laughed.

"Help me, you swine!" howled Dr. Heminglas.

"I'm not allowed to make any decisions, sir," said Lieutenant Duckworth.

Ralph giggled.

"Nonsense! No decision to make. How does five hundred dollars sound?" Dr. Heminglas's fingers gestured over the edge of the hole.

"Dollars?" Lieutenant Duckworth puzzled. "What would I do with them? Have you got a Swiss cheese sandwich on you?"

Dr. Heminglas sputtered, then slipped and fell into the hot cheese again.

"Where to now, Lieutenant?" Dr. Krebnickel asked.

"Well, now I must return exactly the way I came, erasing my path."

"Through my laboratory, in other words."

"Yes, sir. That is true."

"And you really wouldn't mind a couple of passengers," Ralph added as he climbed on back of the motorcycle.

"Well, not really, sir."

"Great. We've got to get the neutrino turbine to the power agency!"

There was just room enough for the three humans. Lieutenant Duckworth started the cycle, and they roared off down the road and right into a black tunnel that suddenly appeared in the mountain.

Dr. Heminglas, eyes just above the edge of the pit, howled.

10: Surprises and Sleep

THE other end of the hole in Mount Hortense came out in Dr. Krebnickel's laboratory. It was a great ride. The hole was like a tube through the Milky Way, with flaming lights everywhere, zipping past. In only a few minutes the patrolcycle roared out into Dr. Krebnickel's lab. There was bright sunlight streaming in the broken windows.

"Hey," Louie said, "we were so busy we didn't notice it's morning."

The light hurt Ralph's eyes.

"Ralph!" Louie said again. "Your hair! It's not very purple anymore. The color is fading."

"Great."

"That is normal," Lieutenant Duckworth said. "Since you have returned through my hole with me."

"My goodness!" Dr. Krebnickel suddenly exclaimed, realizing what time it was. "I have to get my equipment to the power authority. I must activate Quarwyn immediately."

He turned the computer on, but before he could ask Quarwyn anything, the screen began flashing strange colored shapes, like a quilt.

"That's the Hole Control pattern," Lieutenant Duckworth said.

"They called while you were out," Quarwyn buzzed. "On the tachyphone. A very interesting message. They also transported something, over there on the table."

It looked like some sort of trophy, all gold and engraved, with a wooden base.

"It's got your name on it, Ralph," Louie said.

The award looked like a statue of half a cheese sandwich.

"They said it was the Nothingness Award," Quarwyn reported. "For service to the universe by preventing Founder's Day from returning. They sent the other half of the sandwich to Switzerland, about 1909."

"To Dr. Einstein?" Ralph gulped. He shared a prize with Albert Einstein!

"Hear, hear!" Lieutenant Duckworth cheered.

"There is a message for you, too, Lieutenant," Quarwyn said.

"There is? Good heavens, they found out what I've done! I'll be stuck on quark* patrol forever now."

*See Krebnickel's Glossary

"No. You've been promoted to captain. For your bravery in finally deciding."

It was the humans' turn to cheer. But Duckworth only looked more disgusted.

"What terrible news! I suppose they'll want more decisions now. I hate making decisions!"

Captain Duckworth got on his motorcycle, still grumbling, and drove off into the hole in the wall. The hole disappeared and the bookshelf returned.

Dr. Krebnickel and Louie hurriedly screwed the pickle jar back into its mount. Quarwyn turned on the turbine. The machine gasped, then lurched into its familiar hum. Dials all over it spun like crazy. Everything was working perfectly.

They looked up at the long ramp to the back doors. "But I'm supposed to be at the power agency at nine!" Dr. Krebnickel suddenly realized. "We'll never get it into the truck and downtown in twenty minutes."

"Oh, yes, we will," Louie said. "Push, everybody!" He threw all his weight at the bulky turbine.

Fretfully, Dr. Krebnickel helped. The big mass of tubes and wires and gadgets moved forward a little on its tiny wheels.

"C'mon, Ralph!" Louie shouted.

"I'm exhausted, Louie," Ralph whined. "Can't we just call the power agency and tell them you'll be late, Doc?"

"They're very punctual," Dr. Krebnickel sobbed. "They'll never grant me a second demonstration."

Ralph shuffled forward, wishing he had never wanted the H32 helmet for a souvenir. His arms were like empty banana peels. The night had been too long. He really couldn't help.

"Wait a minute!" Quarwyn called. "Professor, look at Ralph's balloon."

"Remarkable."

Ralph looked up. The Hole Control balloon still bobbed from his belt. Ralph blinked.

"Hey! It's gotten bigger!"

It was nearly double its former size. And when Ralph took a step, he noticed he felt lighter.

"What is causing the expansion, Quarwyn?" Dr. Krebnickel said, reaching for his equipment.

"Apparently the gas inside is xenon," the computer announced. "But why it is increasing in volume I cannot tell. Perhaps the neutrinos . . ."

"That's it!" Louie screamed. "The turbine! The hole is pulling in millions of stray neutrinos from the turbine. They're exciting the particles inside the xenon!"

"HELP!" Ralph cried. The balloon was getting a lot bigger, and it was lifting him off the floor.

Louie and the professor jumped for him, but it was too late. Ralph was floating up through the hole in the house. Desperately, he grabbed a pipe on the neutrino turbine and held on.

"Turn it off!" Ralph yelled.

"No, wait," Louie said. "Ralph, see if you can attach the line to the turbine."

"What? I'm floating away, and you want me to do an experiment! I'll kill you when I get out of here!"

"Do as he says, Ralph," the professor encouraged. "I think I understand."

Ralph wound the wire tightly around a big pipe on top of the turbine, muttering. He still couldn't get it loose from his belt. The only thing that happened then was that the balloon continued to grow.

"Okay, what do I do now?" Ralph sneered.

But before anybody could reply, the turbine lurched. One wheel bounced off the floor. The growing balloon was lifting the whole turbine!

Louie cheered. "It's working! Come on, Professor, climb on. Next stop's the Metro Power Agency."

Dr. Krebnickel and Louie clambered up onto the thrumming machine. In no time the expanding xenon had lifted the three of them and the invention out of the lab. Slowly they rose up through Dr. Krebnickel's wrecked house and out the top, just clearing the big oak tree in his front yard. A cool morning breeze met them, and it was blowing in just the right direction.

"Hey, look," Louie said, "everybody can see us."

Ralph peeked over the edge. Louie was right. They were making quite a commotion as they passed over Fogville. All the little people looked like ants as they scurried out of their houses to look up at the strange balloon. The flight caused traffic jams. Ralph and Dr. Krebnickel had to hold Louie down so that he wouldn't make the neutrino turbine rock too much.

Soon the power agency came into view. Dr. Krebnickel cut the power way down on the turbine so the balloon would shrink, and they flew lower and lower. Finally, as they brushed the treetops, Dr. Krebnickel turned the machine off. They had an argument about whether or not to do that. Ralph lost.

Dr. Krebnickel made the biggest entrance anyone had ever made at the Metro Power Agency. His neutrino turbine plunged right through the roof of the building into the meeting room.

Mayor Winklebran pounded frantically for order while shouting, "What is the meaning of this? What is the meaning of this?"

Finally Dr. Krebnickel's gestures for silence were obeyed. He stood on top of the turbine, with the utility board gathered around in the dust and debris, and introduced the neutrino turbine. Louie ran some cables from the turbine to the power agency's monitoring meters, which lined one wall.

Dr. Krebnickel explained all about neutrinos, and how they were speeding through the universe all the time, and how his invention could tap their energy. He got real technical. Most of the utility board started yawning.

That was about the last thing Ralph remembered . . .

. . . until he woke up in his own bed. It was night. For a while he had the really weird feeling it had all just been a dream. But he couldn't find the H32 helmet, and his hair was still faintly purple. He must have just fallen asleep on top of the turbine, he figured, and Dr. Krebnickel couldn't wake him up.

He found out later that Dr. Krebnickel had gotten the contract from the power authority. But only after Dr. Heminglas had shown up at the meeting and tried to get everybody to vote against him. But it didn't work. The neutrino turbine worked great. When Dr. Krebnickel threw the switch, the measuring dials went berserk. Three of them melted. So the vote went to Dr. Krebnickel. Besides, it turned out there was a rule that you had to take your hat off before you voted, and Dr. Heminglas's hat was stuck on with melted cheese. He smelled like a pizza. Mayor Winklebran yelled at him about his eating habits and threw him out of the meeting.

Dr. Krebnickel took Ralph home, and he slept for twenty-two hours straight. He slept through his father's towing the house back to the place it had been the night before. Louie called him the next day and told him everything.

Louie tried to come over after that, but every time he did, Ralph climbed out of his bedroom window and hid in a tree. Louie called and called in the backyard, but finally left with whatever new gadget he had brought.

One day a package for Ralph arrived from Dr. Krebnickel. The postmark was Switzerland, where the professor was vacationing after his lecture at the museum. It was an old photograph of Albert Einstein, along with a letter. It was fuzzy like all pictures that old, but there was something funny about Einstein's hair . . . even in black-and-white you could tell it was purple. Ralph threw away the letter, which had a lot of equations in it. But he framed the picture.

It was nice and boring in the tree. It was going to be a nice boring summer for Ralph Fozbek.

Krebnickel's Glossary

Andromeda—A constellation, which is a pattern of stars. This one is supposed to be in the shape of a lady. The nearest galaxy to ours is in this constellation. But Dr. Krebnickel's black hole is there only in this story.

Big bang—The explosion that started the universe. There was once a big ball of stuff, and something made it blow up and spread throughout space, forming galaxies and planets and stars as it got cooler.

Black hole—A black hole is not really a hole at all. It is a star, a really big one that gets so heavy that it shrinks. All its atoms scrunch closer and closer together, and that makes its gravity stronger. Finally its gravity is so strong that nothing is stronger. Light can't even get away from the star, so it looks like a big black spot in space. Black holes can be tiny in size, but nobody can trap them in pickle jars like Dr. Krebnickel—yet.

Declination—Imaginary lines on the sky, which astronomers use to locate stars. It's like longitude on a map.

Electrons—Tiny particles of light that race around inside atoms. When electrons line up and run, they make electricity.

Gravity wave—A disturbance in gravity, kind of like an earthquake in space-time. Scientists are looking for gravity waves, but so far haven't found any real ones.

Infrared—In the spectrum, infrared is the color right after red. You'll never see it, because it's invisible to our eyes. Some telescopes can see infrared, and some stars are brighter in infrared than any other color.

Neutrino—A particle formed when a neutron gets radioactive. The neutron is part of an atom. The neutrino doesn't weigh anything, and nothing can stop it. Billions of them are going through you this very minute. I don't know how Dr. Krebnickel could get them to turn a turbine, but if you could get a black hole into a pickle jar it would probably be easy.

Quark—Very weird little things which scientists call by names like Color and Strange and Beauty. They are the forces which make atoms possible.

Radio galaxy—Really, two galaxies, bumping into each other. When they do that, they make a lot of microwave noise, and can be heard all over the universe, if you have the right ears, like Quarwyn and Bertha.

Right ascension—Imaginary lines on the sky, like declination lines, but these are like latitude.

Tachyon—A particle which cannot slow down to the speed of light. It can only go faster than light. Scientists think they exist, but can't find one. If they could find one, they might be able to make a tachyphone like Dr. Krebnickel's that makes calling across the universe a cinch.

Time warp—What could happen if some force, such as crazy black hole gravity, or travel at the speed of light, bent time out of shape. Then you might fall through a tear in time, and go back millions of years.

White dwarf—A star that has become very tiny, but very bright. All its atoms are compressed. If the star gets any sicker, it could become a black hole.